Blind

Date

Tails

FOR LITERARY HEAT

www.BarbarianSpy.com

BarbarianSpy
Toronto, NSW
Australia

Blind Date

Tails

by

Shabbu

Table of Contents

Introduction

Gay male blind dating can be a real crap shoot, resulting in pleasure, humor, rejection, surprise, success, and/or defeat, whether initiated through an Internet dating service or referrals by friends. The motivation for engaging in blind dating can be curiosity, need, laziness, or a sense of adventure and for the bizarre. In this anthology of gay male blind date stories, American author, habu, from the U.S. East Coast, and his Aussie coauthor, Sabb, now writing from southern Europe, have combined in their pen name Shabbu to explore and entertain with this form of hookup hunting. The two authors are compatible in writing style but are very different in their story styles, Sabb being more gentle, hopeful, and romantic with his characters and outcomes and habu being rougher and more cynical, graphic, visceral with his. But all of these stories, which provide highly varied settings, motivations, and unfolding, have one thing in common—they all culminate in a sexual hookup, something which, if participants are being honest, is the goal of blind dating but in far too many cases not the result. Three of the stories have previously been published in habu anthologies, but nine appear here for the first time.

Sabb has contributed five of the twelve stories in the anthology. His first story, "Taken to Church," describes a fleeting hookup between an American tourist visiting Galicia, Spain, to visit historical churches there and the Spanish guide he contracted through a gay travel site. "Clay and Jose" speaks to the steam of the chocolate and vanilla image overshadowing the need to resolve the top/bottom agreement. The arrangement in "Nathan and Jack's Blind Date," works out despite an misunderstanding of why the two men have been brought together.

Sabb's "Japaneseartlover," another almost-botched Internet dating service hookup, is somewhat of an "in" joke between Sabb and habu, as the subject—beyond scoring on a blind date—is collecting mid-twentieth-century Japanese woodblock prints, and it is habu, not Sabb, who collects this art. In Sabb's concluding story, "Blame it on the GPS," a blind date is used to bring two old misunderstanding lovers back together again.

Seven of the stories in the anthology have been provided by habu. The first, "Ted and Zach's Blind Date," is of a surprise, athletic, interracial workout on what started as two failed dates with other men. In the previously published "The Blind Date," a blind date arranged for revenge both shows that first impressions can be faulty and turns out to be ideal. "My First Black" moves back in time from a furtive, "make us forget" coupling in war-torn Vietnam to a memory of a first blind date of a white civil rights worker with a black bull in the South of 1964. The previously published "Tight Squeeze" offers up a no-holds-barred rough sex, bondage, BDSM blind date of a thirties dominator with a twenties submissive. "Public Warrior Dating" shows how dating firemen and policemen off Craigslist can make for an adventuresome date.

A previously published habu story, "Three on a Date," has a bored, young Smithsonian Institute curator finding an Internet dating service for threesomes and then just about more than he can handle. Habu's concluding story, "Doubled Date," shows what can happen when two bottoms go on a shared blind date with two tops who like to double.

Ted and Zack's Blind Date

The sound of the toilet flushing took my attention away from the soft melody of the music in the background, not quite loud enough for me to recognize the tune, but something for me to try to concentrate on in my nervousness. I had no idea why I had agreed to this, why I was here.

It was a studio apartment, but the room was large. There was a living and dining area and even an exercise corner where I saw that he had parallel bars, both set low to the ground, the nearer at waist level and the one beyond that about a foot and a half lower. I shuddered at the thought of how he might use those.

Over in the far corner was the kitchen area, separated from the bigger room by a table-high, marble-topped counter. The marble had been cold. This is where he'd fucked me in the second and third positions the first time, starting with my legs folded against his hips, him palming and separating my buttocks, my torso reclining back toward that counter with my arms stiff and the heels of my hands pressing into the countertop to hold my body steady as he fucked me. He'd said he like an athletic fuck. It certainly had been that.

He also had said that he liked to have his partner doing the splits when he fucked him. We had gotten naked and he flopped down on his sofa and pulled me down on my knees between his spread thighs, obviously wanting a blow job, which I gave him, my teeth having trouble not clicking against the thick ring in the bulb of his cock. Then he pulled me up on the couch and we cuddled, rather belatedly, I thought, in some exploratory first-date fondling, which progressed to my being on my back against the arm of the sofa, my left leg crossing his chest, the ankle hooked on his shoulder, and him finger fucking me to an ejaculation.

After that he introduced splits fucking to me, starting with a cowboy splits position with him sitting in the middle of the sofa and me straddling his hips, facing him, and riding his cock, with my legs stretched straight out to either side in the splits and him holding my sides in his hands and fucking up into my ass. Then, without coming, he carried me, showing off how strong he was, to the kitchen counter, fucking me in the second position suspended in front of the counter and then in the third position before coming, facing the kitchen, my legs in the splits, my hands pressed into the cold marble in front of me, his hands pressing down on my knee joints to keep me in the splits position, and finished the first fuck by taking me from behind.

I had been completely submissive for him. He had made total submissiveness a condition for bringing me home with him, and I had wanted this fuck. He had wanted to fuck me with me doing the splits, and both of those positions certainly had been me doing the splits for him.

So was this. I was on my back on his bed, a wedge pillow under the small of my back, rolling my pelvis up. My legs were pulled straight from my sides, in the splits, and bound at the ankles on both sides of the bed, where he had a four-column metal stand, two columns each side, that joined under the bed. My arms were similarly stretched straight out from my body and tied off at the wrists on the other two columns.

I had agreed to be bound before he agreed to bring me here. I had wanted it badly. I had wanted it totally, and I had wanted it with the inventiveness and the challenge to flexibility he had described to me.

I turned my head to the nightstand and saw the used condom, thick as a sea slug, laying on a paper towel. He had said there would be three laying there, in a row, before he was done. I had had the image in my mind all the time he was driving me here.

The door to the bathroom opened and he strode out—all six and a half solidly built, muscular, hard-bodied feet of him, a handsome, black bull hunk. And a virile, vigorous stud as I had already found out and was promised more of. He was holding the base of his erect jet-black cock in one hand and rolling a condom on it with the other. He'd said he was eight inches long and an inch and a half thick, and I had no reason to doubt that from watching it as he moved toward me. He certainly was built big enough otherwise for that to be in proportion.

I did know that it had filled me and challenged me and stretched me—and satisfied me. My first black bull. I already had gotten what I'd hoped for from him, and more, and he wasn't finished with me yet.

He was smiling—a friendly smile and, I hoped, a smile of satisfaction with how this was going. I certainly was doing all I could to make it pleasurable for him. I hadn't said no to any of his demands.

"So, are we ready to go again?" he asked, as he came up on the foot of the bed on his knees.

I didn't say no to this either.

He pushed his knees under my buttocks, positioning the bulb of his cock inside my now-gaping hole, grabbed my hips, thrust inside me, and immediately began to pump.

I gave a little cry at the sudden, deep penetration, groaning and shuddering on how expertly he was working me. Leaning over my torso, he took my mouth with his in a French kiss—and without losing the rhythm of the fuck.

There had been no preparation this time, and there was unlikely to be any the next time. He did say he would have three ejaculations from anal penetrative sex—he would have sounded clinical when he said stuff like this if he didn't say it with such conviction and seriousness—and I could have as many ejaculations of any type as I could manage. He estimated six, which almost made me hyperventilate as assuring as his claim was. I'd never had more than two in a session before. I'd already had two, and so I certainly couldn't say this wasn't good for me. There'd been preparation the first time, but it wasn't needed now. I had been reamed to his requirements in the first twenty-minute fuck. I'd never had a black bull the length and girth of legends before, and he affirmed the legends. He'd said he could fuck vigorously at length, and he hadn't lied. He'd also said he recovered quickly. That too proved to be true.

I now knew what they meant when they talked of black bulls.

He was using his cock to give me another orgasm, pulling the bulb out to my prostate and worrying that before causing me to jerk and arch my back to the extent I could and unsuccessfully try to break his kiss so that I could scream when he dove deep again and revolved inside me, giving attention to all of my walls with that thick ring he had in the bulb of the cock.

And, suspending my writhing, to tense up and break away from the kiss at last to gasp and cry out my release, I came again. As long as he made me come again and again like this, I was his.

"Three," he said. He said he could provide six. I no longer doubted he could. He said it was the reward for giving him what he wanted. My balls already ached from the evacuation of three. I could only shudder at the thought of how drained I would feel after six.

He had told me that this would take no more than two hours from start to finish. I wondered if he'd ask me to spend the night or kick me out after I'd taken a shower and there were three sea-slug-thick used condoms lined up on the paper towel on the top of his nightstand.

I didn't know if I'd be able to walk if he didn't invite me to stay the night. But then I thought of how he would be rejuvenated enough to want it all over again in the morning. I groaned in fear—but also couldn't deny the surge of energy that went through my body in anticipation of getting all of this again—his exotic fetishes; his hard, muscular body; his virility and vigor; his eight-inch, thick cock working my passage; the feel of running my hands over the hard muscles of his chocolate-brown skin. The thrill of my first black bull.

Stretched out and bound like this, all of my sensations concentrated on my channel and that churning cock. He'd said that would help me jack off repeatedly— that he'd take me to heaven repeatedly. I thought he was probably right. I could feel the next orgasm coming on already.

"Four," he sounded out twenty seconds later. "At this rate you could have eight, although I seriously doubt you can produce that much cum in the time given," he cheerfully and helpfully added, his voice floating out over my deep groan. "Ever had a dry jack off?" he asked. "They can roll on and on and be really intense. Hang in there; you're doin' great. You take the positions great and have a sweet ass. Keepin' my pecker real hard here. Doin' your job."

My answering groan was even deeper.

* * * *

Josh had let me get to the restaurant before calling me to say that something had come up and he couldn't make our date. I answered the call outside on the walk between the parking lot and the building and hesitated after the call, but I decided to go on in even though I was alone. I had to eat anyway, and I certainly was in the mood for something to drink. They sat me in the last booth but one in the back corner of the restaurant a few steps up from the bar. I ordered a bourbon chicken something or other appetizer and a beer. I was more thirsty than hungry.

I had some thinking to do. Josh had been in a snit since he'd asked me to move in with him and I said that I needed to think about it.

"What's to think about?" he'd asked. "We have a good thing going."

The problem was that I wasn't sure about the good thing going. I was frightened at the prospect of a monogamous relationship with one man who I'd see every day and sleep with solely. Josh was nearly thirty, obviously ready to settle down. I was barely twenty-one and was still experimenting. I had a "so many cocks and so little time" attitude. The issue went beyond the settled relationship concept, though. Josh was OK as a lover. He was built and on the border of being hung, and he was good looking, had a good job, and was generous with his money. I didn't know whether I was ready to be a kept man, though, and, truth be told, my experimentation had told me that I preferred someone more forceful, demanding, and inventive than Josh was. And I liked variety.

On the other hand, he was there when I needed to be fucked, and I did like to be fucked. When he got wound up, he became demanding, and I liked that too. I liked being controlled and forced—a bit more of that than Josh did, though.

I'd just about finished the chicken and had ordered another beer when a couple of guys were brought to the last booth down the line, which was behind me.

As they passed, I got a glimpse, first, of a slightly under height—like me—guy about my age, who was slim, dressed neatly, and walked gracefully, with a shy demeanor. I got the impression of a dark, sultry, Mediterranean look, which is how my friends often described me as well. The other guy was quite a contrast. He was built like a football player and was a deep chocolate brown. His features were more Caribbean than African in origin, and he strode along the aisle toward me with self-confidence, legs parted like he had a load between his thighs.

He and I made eye contact as they passed and his smile caused me to smile back and incline my head. There was something commanding about him that made me lower my head to him as if in submission. I recognized a dominator when I saw one, and it sent chills up my spine when I readily recognized him as one.

The white guy slipped into the seat backing on mine and the black guy went into the seat across the table from him. They ordered quickly. Their initial conversation, which I clearly could hear but no one else around us could, was on the food choices and their preferences until they had ordered. The white guy had a twangy tenor voice, I could tell by where it projected from, and the black guy more of a smooth, confident baritone. Ours being the last booths in the line there really was no one else nearby except when the waitress came by to deliver or check on the patrons. Next up from my booth was a drinks station, not another booth.

After the waitress took their order, they traded information on what part of town they lived in and whether in a rental apartment, a condo, or a house. The white guy was in a rental with two other guys; the black guy owned his own studio condo. The impression was established that the black guy made quite a bit more money than the white one did. They compared electronics and the white guy came out on the losing end of that. They briefly talked sports. The black guy followed college football, admitting that he'd played it in college on scholarship; the white guy followed pro basketball. He was enrolled at a local college. Religion was tossed out there, but wisely, I thought, dropped immediately. The black guy believed in sleeping in on Sunday mornings—preferably with a bed partner. "I like white tail on a Sunday morning," he said.

He'd obviously thrown that out as an ice-breaking joke, although, as far as I knew, he was speaking the truth. He laughed at his joke; so did the white guy, but nervously and insincerely, and I'd heard the intake of breath from just behind my head. If the black guy was trying to cut to the chase, this should do it. It was Saturday night. The conversation on that stopped when the white guy said he was an Evangelical Baptist.

I realized at that point that these two guys were either meeting for the first time to do some sort of business or were on a blind date. If the latter, I thought, the religion issue should be enough to end the conversation and close out the date early—unless the white guy really wanted to be laid by a black stud, in which case they could fold up their tent now and get to it.

The "what do you see yourself doing in five years" question that next came up made me think they were strangers considering doing business together, and I was intrigued enough—and bored enough and at loose ends enough—to order another beer when the waitress came with my tab. The "five years" question was one I associated with dating, but the black guy responded in terms of business. He said he was a stock broker and hoped to have his own branch of his firm within the five years. The white guy, who was referred to as Ted, was still in college but also was a private high school—the Baptists again, apparently—

gym assistant teacher. He saw himself as a vice principal in that time.

He also saw himself settled down in a steady relationship by then.

Then it became evident that the meeting wasn't about business.

"Oh, I don't think I will be," Zack, the black guy said. "Five years from now I think I'll still be moving around. I like to experience what there is out there— variety. Different kinds of guys, cruising like me, but they have to be fit."

There was a bit of silence here and Zack picked up the conversation. "The gym angle was what caught my eye. And your age. I like dating younger guys. You look like you're in great shape, and you walked loose, like you're really flexible. I like that. You look like a gymnast."

"You're built too—more so than I am," Ted answered. "You must spend half your free time in the gym. You've got great guns and definition."

I'd noticed that too when I'd glanced at the black guy. He was dressed conservatively enough, but the way his clothes fit him accentuated his cut musculature. There was no surprise he'd played football in college.

"I *am* a gymnast," Ted continued. "I took the fifth year at Temple to help the varsity team."

"Bet you can do the splits all the way down," Zack said, to which Ted answered in the affirmative.

I was really interested in the conversation now. First, obviously this was a blind date and the two were feeling each other out. They were gay. They were my kind of men. That piqued my interest right there. Beyond that, I was a gymnast too—but at U. Penn, so I didn't recognize this guy. Temple wasn't on U. Penn's level. And, I thought with a bit of bravado, I probably could do the splits all the way down better than this Temple guy could.

My beer was half down, but I decided to nurse it. These guys were getting into more intimate talk, and maybe I'd find it arousing. My date with Josh was supposed to have ended in bed, and even if we were having a rough time in our relationship, I still was in the need of a fuck. Josh could be upset with me and still fuck me. It might even make the fuck more exciting.

"A gym teacher in a private school, eh. I guess that means you aren't out yet."

"No. You?"

"Sure. I think it makes me more interesting. It certainly makes cruising easier. So, was the file right? You like to take cock?"

I nearly choked on the swig of beer I was drinking when he said that.

A bit of silence preceded Ted's response. "Well, I've done it both ways."

"I only give cock," Zack answered. "I think it said that on my profile."

"Yes, it does," Ted answered.

I felt a little warm at that—at Zack's part of the discussion becoming pretty bald. I'll take your cock, I thought, feeling the buzz of the second beer. I found that my hand had gone to my crotch and that it had found more than the usual mounding there. No way I was going anywhere as long as this conversation was spinning out.

"You pretty active?"

"Not really. But one gets curious, you know—wants to expand the circle of friends he's comfortable with." Ted was sounding like he was forming what he had to say carefully. "What about you?"

"Oh, you know, I fuck who I can when I can. They've got to be athletic, though—and submissive. I have my fetishes. So, are you the adventure and risk-taking kind? That wasn't clear on your profile."

"Do you mean do I go down on the first date? Or do I bareback?" Ted's voice sounded tight.

"Well, I don't do bareback—I go with too many guys. But, yes, do you fuck on the first date?"

I strained to hear Ted's answer, but the waitress showed up just then to ask if I wanted anything else. I guess she was goosing me to pay my tab and clear the table. I ordered another beer, gulping the last couple of swallows in the one I had and giving the glass back to her.

When I could listen in again, it was sort of a shocking monologue from the black guy—I wanted to think of him as a black bull now, having heard the legends about black bulls and not having tried one yet, and he affirmed that right fast.

"A guy laying under me needs to be able to take eight inches hard—and, probably more important—an inch and a half thick."

I had visions of Ted sitting there with his mouth hanging open in what he was being told he had to look forward to. Josh had told me that he was a little more than seven hard and thick—although he didn't tell me how thick. And I was always begging him to give me more. So, eight inches—that would be a challenge, I would think—and something to look forward to.

"And the gymnast part that caught my eye. I use challenging positions. My favorite is putting my partner in the splits to fuck him. I have a set of useful parallel bars for that in my condo. And stamina. I can fuck twenty minutes at a time. I need a guy who will keep with me—and who doesn't mind being bound during sex. And I have rituals. I do it three times with a rubber in a session, if I like the guy and he is completely submissive to me. I'll give him five or six jack offs, but I get three with a rubber from the anal sex alone. I'll come more often if the other guy gives good blow jobs, but only the ones earned inside a hole and wearing a rubber count officially. And I line my used

21

rubbers up as I finish as some sort of victory celebration. Oh, and I have a Prince Albert—a PA, thick ring in my cock head. You've been fucked by a guy with a PA before, haven't you?"

I couldn't help myself. I swiveled my head to get another look at this guy. And I got a very clear look, because he now was the only guy in the booth. He'd been talking to the back of my head. Ted was gone—he must have left while I was talking to the waitress.

What in the hell was all that added sexy stuff for? It had made me hard and dripping.

"Don't turn back, sweetheart," Zack said—clearly and directly to me. "Come on over into my booth—beside me, not across from me—and I'll stand you a drink and jack off your cock. Ever been done in a busy restaurant before?"

He had me at "come over into my booth" even though I considered the part about jacking me off in the restaurant as bravado. "But Ted—the other guy?"

"He left after the 'would he fuck on the first date?' question. I've been talkin' to you since then, not him. I knew it wasn't to be as soon as he told me he was a Holy-Roller Baptist. I recognize you. I've seen you at some gymnastic events at U. Penn. I know you can do splits, and I know that you stuck to your booth there to listen to us talk. I'm also friends with Niles, on your gymnastics team. He says you're a great lay. I didn't think I'd ever manage to get rid of that loser I'd been hooked up with. Come on over. No, slide in here beside me."

As I slid into the booth, he had one arm snaking around my shoulder and the other hand went straight to my crotch.

"Hmm, I can tell you already want me. I don't have to ask you if you take cock on the first date, do I?"

He proved me wrong about not jacking me off right there in the restaurant, making good use of one of the restaurant's extra paper napkins.

* * * *

Showing me the strength he had, I was draped on Zack's front, my legs hooked on his slightly crouched thighs to counterbalance my back being arched back, his arms embracing me around my waist, his teeth chewing lightly on my nipples, and my channel being bounced up and down on his cock when I shot my fifth load.

"Five!" he called out. "Moving right along."

When I had ejaculated up his belly, he turned and frog marched me over to the parallel bars that I had been nervously eyeing for the hour and a half so far of this fascinating, invigorating fuck.

"Do the splits on the higher, nearer bar," he commanded, "and arch back to the lower bar, neck on that towel wrapped around the bar and arms at a stretch. Open to me totally."

I did as he directed, He pulled out of me long enough to lash my ankles in the splits to the higher bar and then returned and thrust his sheathed cock inside my channel and glided his hands down my inclined and stretched torso and latching onto my nipples with pinching fingers.

"I like my men in the splits on the first date when I fuck them," he said, which I'd already heard him say more than once, "but on subsequent dates I like to get more athletic. They have to give me everything."

I shuddered at the thought—at the scary thought— at the divine thought. I was getting exactly what I had been pining for that my relationship with Josh wasn't giving me.

Five times. He'd exploded me over the moon five times. I'd walk on fire for a man who could give me five orgasms in one fuck session—even though it was sucking everything out of me and making my balls ache.

He nailed my ass again strongly and immediately began to pump. We were long past me needing time to open to him. He did me so well that I knew I'd open right up for him in the future just seeing him swagger toward me. The PA in his cock was caressing my walls, setting my muscles undulating, and driving me crazy for the fuck. He pumped on for some twenty minutes—I think he had an internal clock with the time set—periodically leaning over me to kiss and nibble at my nipples and to bring my head up for a kiss.

At the finish, he brought my torso up into a close embrace, covered me with kisses, stuck his tongue down my throat and gave me several long, deep strokes.

Wham! I came again. He released my mouth and muttered, "Six for you," and then Bang! He tensed, jerked, cried out an "Oh, shit, Yes!" and filled the bulb of his third condom.

"And three for me in the ass!"

We remained like that for a few minutes, him embracing me, my legs still in bound splits on the higher rail.

"Do you do overnights and repeated fucks on the first date?" he whispered in my ear.

"Yes," I replied.

"You're a great first date. Niles was right. You're a great lay, up for anything I want to take out of you. You won't get all clutchy on me now, will you? It's just a fuck session. I'll call you to come to regularly, but you're not moving in with me."

I trembled at the "call you to come" to me statement. Master and slave. He could have me any time he wanted me.

"No." All I wanted was that eight-inch cock of his with the ring in the bulb churning inside me from time to time and, Wham-Bang, six jack-offs in a session. I didn't want to marry him.

"What will you let me do to you on a second date?"

"You bury that black cock in me to the hilt and give me multiple orgasms and you can do anything you want to me," I answered.

Considering he proceeded to give me a seventh orgasm—and one of those balls aching rolling on and on dry orgasms—before we slept, I must have given him the right answer.

Taken to Church

Once the plane had taken off and he could relax, Lance made himself comfortable in his business-class seat and closed his eyes, remembering.

* * * *

Javier threw a leg over Lance's hip, an arm around his head, and pretended to wrestle him. He was enjoying the feel of skin on skin, their bodies moving against each other, the struggle going on for a few minutes and becoming ever-more intimate. A hand on a cock, a knee between thighs, a tongue licking the skin at a neck, a leg rubbing against a stiffening dick. The game ended with Lance on top, as he usually was, holding Javier's arms spread, with his knees between Javier's bent legs.

Javier wrapped his calves around Lance's waist and laughed. Lance smiled down into his lover's half-closed eyes and felt himself swallowed up by them, as his cock would shortly be swallowed by Javier's hole.

Lance held Javier's eyes as his hard cock made its way into Javier's entrance and slid in deep with little effort. It had been a lazy, sex-filled afternoon on the veranda of the small stone cottage overlooking the river. Javier was ready for him, taking him in as if he was fitting together two parts of one whole. A slick, well-oiled piston in its cylinder, starting to move in and out, gathering speed and then slowing as they moved along the road to mutual satisfaction. Lance had released one of Javier's arms so his hand could go to his cock, a nice size and thick, a handful and more, stroking it in tune with the rhythm of the fuck.

They came together and collapsed, lying exhausted and aching, well drained and totally satisfied.

* * * *

"So do you go every Sunday?" Lance had asked the first time they met.

"Yes, for me it's important. And you, why are you going?"

"I want to see the churches, to get a feel for the history of them, and the best way is to attend a mass in them as that is when the atmosphere is best. Many are only open for mass anyway." Lance hesitated. "I also . . . find that I like to feel part of the tradition. Knowing that I am included in something that has been happening in much the same way in the same place for four hundred, five hundred, maybe even eight hundred or a thousand years. But I often do not understand what is going on so . . ."

"You want a companion who can explain things to you?"

"Yes. Yes, so the church we are going to today, what can you tell me about it?"

"It is small and very primitive. The small church is attached to a convent that was originally founded in 967 and then fell into disuse and was reopened in 1676."

That had been their first meeting, breakfast in a café by the old convent church in the small medieval town, and then they had attended the mass. When it was over they walked to the car park together before parting.

"I must go now, Sunday lunch is sometimes a big family event . . . and today is one of those. But next Sunday? You want to go to the church by the castle on the hill?" Javier asked as they walked back to their cars.

"Yes. Breakfast too?"

"I suppose so. There is a nice café in the hotel next to the church."

"Ah, yes, in what was originally the convent attached to the church."

Lance watched Javier drive off and then took a scenic route back to his hotel. In the church he had concentrated on what was going on and in studying the primitive carvings, listening to the old nuns sing in their broken voices as they heard mass from behind the cast-iron screen that separated them from the congregation—a congregation of six people, including Lance and Javier. But the chapel would only have held fifty people even if each seat had been occupied. Small and intimate.

Now he could think of Javier sexually, though, of knowing him intimately, which was very satisfying.

The following Sunday they had gone to the café in the adjoining hotel for breakfast and then to the mass. Javier had explained that this church was not as old as the one the week before, but it was much larger and had been designed by a well-known Madrid-based architect of the late 1600s.

When the mass was over, the setting having been breathtaking and the priest chanting much of the mass adding to the splendor and otherworldyness of it, Lance watched Javier walk away down the hill, finally letting himself think of him in another way. It had been wrong to do it up to then. Not in church, certainly.

* * * *

They had taken a room in the hotel that had once been a convent next to the castle and lay side by side on the bed after fucking, arms lying touching each other's and hands clasped.

"How do you balance the Catholic Church being important in your life with being gay?" Lance asked. It was something that had been on his mind since they had first set up a meeting. He often thought of it as a blind date, as they had met through a gay dating site.

Javier shrugged. "God himself gave me my body and my urges, so I do not question them."

"But the Church . . ."

"The Church? Men trying to interpret what God wants, and satisfy their own desires, they are not God."

Lance asked no more. Javier had found his way to reconcile himself with his religion. Instead, Lance ran a hand down Javier's belly to his bush and stroked his cock and felt his balls, moving his hand between Javier's thighs so they parted and Javier gave a little sigh. Lance moved a finger further, to Javier's rim, and Javier bent his legs and spread them, a hand going to Lance's chest and moving over it lazily as the finger moved into his channel. Then there were two fingers slowly moving in and out searching for Javier's prostrate. Lance's cock was filling out in tune with Javier's, their breathing getting louder and the heat in the room building.

It was Javier who wanted it first, turning over and straddling Lance's hips and riding Lance's cock, looking down into his face and raising his arms up as if in a homage to God for what he was receiving, before letting his hands fall and rest on Lance's shoulders.

The next Sunday the mass was too late for breakfast, but they met for coffee before and crossed the Roman bridge together to the wealthy city convent founded in the late 1600s. They entered a church that obviously belonged to women. The convent was also obviously wealthy and old hand cut crystal chandeliers and finely carved confessionals decorated its well-cared-for interior.

Again there were nuns, but now hidden in an upper gallery. It was Lance's last Sunday in Galicia, his last Sunday before flying home to the States.

Their last lovemaking in Lance's hotel room was passionate and heated. The sense of loss, of something special ending making it more intense. Almost painful.

The kisses were deep with a desire to make them more memorable, the hands roaming over bodies, as with closed eyes they sought to capture the feel and shape of each other. The sex was a final releasing and capturing of seed, a holding of the moment of each ejaculation to remember it as different from others.

Finally, they fucked in an exhausted dreamy way, skin on skin. Their shared sex being their whole world, neither Lance or Javier wanting to think of tomorrow.

The Blind Date

"Whoa, is that a photo you're shredding on your dart board?"

"Yeah, what's it to you?" Lionel Nicks walked over to the board, took the five darts out, and went back to the other side of the bar in his apartment.

"Peace, big guy. I was just asking." Andre Sanders took a closer look at the photo. "Say, isn't that Devin? Your Devin? You guys no longer a couple?" He didn't bother not sounding hopeful.

"Devin, dear Devin, decided we should cool it. Should see other people. Said he wanted to date around. That we just weren't clicking right. Stand away, if you don't want to be needled."

Andre backed off from the board as Lionel scored a hit right between Devin's eyes.

"I'd like to see that Devin gets a date around or two he'd never forget." Zing went another dart.

Andre thought for a moment. "I might be able to help with that . . . if . . ."

"If what, Andre?"

"Seeing as how you two aren't an item anymore— that you're as free now as Devin is . . . well, you know I was after you to fuck me before you hooked up with Devin and claimed a one-and-only arrangement. I'm still interested. And, you know, I'm the equipment manager of the Triangle Nighthawks."

"Yeah, how does being a semipro football team's equipment manager have anything to do with this?"

Andre told him.

* * * *

Andre had told Devin the guy would meet him at the Tracks bar out on the edge of Benson, near the stadium where the North Carolina league semipro football team, the Triangle Nighthawks, played. A wide receiver for the rival East Carolina Rams who was a friend of Andre's was in town to scout the Nighthawks in a game and had asked Andre not only to get him tickets to the game on the sly— Andre shouldn't be helping a rival team—but also to line up a date to go to the game with him. Andre well knew the guy's preferences. Andre's ass still hurt from that knowing.

"I heard you were dating and open to a blind date," he said when he pitched Devin about going out on a blind date with one of his friends.

"Yeah, I might be interested. I'd just meet him at the game and sit with him?"

"He'd stand you a dinner too," Andre said. "He'd meet you at Tracks and take you to dinner before the game."

"OK, that sounds cool."

"He's black. I may have forgotten to mention that. You have any trouble having a blind date with a black guy?" Andre was black. What could Devin say, no matter what he felt if he didn't want to insult Andre? Truth be told he hadn't thought about how he should feel about being seen with a black guy.

"No, I guess not. Haven't dated a black guy before. But a drink, dinner, and the game? No problem."

"Sure. That's it."

When Devin entered Tracks, he was wondering if he'd recognize the guy. The bar was pretty crowded—mostly with other guys going to the game—almost all guys. It was a gay bar. He shouldn't have worried about picking him out, though. A black guy was rising—and rising and rising—from a table and waving to him. Andre had said he'd give a photo of Devin to the guy—in fact, he had done so in arranging the blind date with the guy. Devin hadn't been shown a photo of his blind date, but he had no trouble picking him out of the crowd.

The football player, Marcus Black, was hard to miss and couldn't have been more different from Devin. Marcus was at least ten inches taller than Devin's five foot seven, and seemingly as wide across the chest as Devin was tall. And he was built like a Sherman tank, coming in at close to two-hundred pounds, at the top of the range for a wide receiver. He outweighed a willowy, twinky Devin, with his curly blond hair and face more pretty than handsome by fifty-five pounds. Devin felt like a dwarf in coming up beside him. His hand disappeared in Marcus' at the handshake, and he steeled himself for the grasp to be crushing. But it wasn't. It was firm enough, but it also was gentle—almost caressing.

"Devin?" The smile was broad, friendly. The face had been beaten about but had arrived into something that was ruggedly handsome and honest. The voice a smooth baritone, promising cultured diction. Devin had been told Marcus hailed from the tidewater of Virginia and had graduated from the posh College of William and Mary, in colonial Williamsburg, but he was still surprised at how smooth and sophisticated the man appeared to be.

He was elegantly dressed too. Yet another surprise. Devin hadn't been sure how to dress for a minor league football game in the summer. Devin went to concerts and plays. He watched pro football games on TV just like everyone else, but he did it mainly to watch the big bruisers' butts in their tight-fitting football pants. It's not that Devin was a pansy—not by any means. He worked out, he worked hard at looking clean cut. He just was a happy bottom in private. Not a promiscuous one, though—he'd been satisfied with Lionel at the start. He wasn't sure what had made him a little restless. It could have been the writing he'd been doing—and managing to sell through an erotic publisher.

So, when it came to dress, Devin had decided to wear khakis and a checked sports shirt and loafers without socks. He'd brought a sweater as he didn't know if it would turn cool in the stadium in the evening. He had this reversed on his back, with the sweater arms tied across his chest. For him, preppy was always in season. If it was preppy from the sixties, he didn't care. He knew he looked cool and twinky.

He'd half expected Marcus to come in cutoff jeans and a sweatshirt. But he was wearing pressed slacks, a fitted white shirt that obviously was expensive, and a camel-hair sports coat. He had on boots, but they were black shiny leather polished to a mirror sheen and rose just a bit higher than his ankles. Of course his feet were enormous—boats. As was everything else about him—his hands, his thighs in the tailored slacks, the bulges of his chest and biceps . . . and the bulge at his crotch. But he had the grace of a dancer at the same time, an attribute, Devin assumed, of having to dance down the football field and pull in a guided missile. One would think that his dreadlocks, the tips of which reached his shoulders and were capped with gold metal clips, would belie the rest of his appearance, but the whole package was so neat that they seemed a natural accompaniment.

They sat, chatting, over their drinks, at the table. Devin had expected beer, but Marcus ordered a vodka martini, so he felt comfortable enough to order a

Manhattan on the rocks. He normally would have been embarrassed to do so in the presence of someone he didn't know well, but he felt completely comforting in ordering a cocktail in this situation. In fact, his whole expectation of what going on a blind date with a black football player would be like was being exploded.

"So, I hear you are a hairdresser."

"Yes," Devin answered, ready for the inevitable follow-on stereotyping comments. Maybe he'd been wrong to order a Manhattan.

"That must pay well, and is probably a pretty creative field," Marcus said without a hint of sarcasm or judgment in his voice. "I wouldn't have imagined you to be that if I just saw you on the street."

"Oh, what would you think I was?" Devin asked. No, he knew he didn't appear effeminate. No he didn't have the mannerisms and flamboyance everyone seemed to expect of a gay hairdresser. Still, here he was, drinking a Manhattan.

"Oh, a college student, or maybe a young stage actor or male model. Andre said you were twenty. I can hardly believe it, seeing you in person."

So, what was he saying, Devin wondered—that Devin looked too young to be in a bar and Marcus that he be nabbed for buying liquor for a minor? Or was he saying he liked them young enough to seem illegal? From looking into Marcus' face, he couldn't get a hint that this wasn't more than just ice-breaking chit chat.

"Yes, all of twenty," he answered. "Twenty and a couple of weeks."

"I'm twenty-eight. Getting old for football. If I don't make it up to the pros this season, I might have to hang up that dream."

"And do what?"

"I have an architectural degree and my family has a construction firm in its portfolio. I have a financial

35

parachute. That makes pursuing the dream of football easier."

"Don't you have to go longer than normal for a degree like that? Isn't that like an advanced degree?"

"Yes, I went for six years."

"Wow." He wasn't anything like Devin imagined. His speech had been as sophisticated as Devin first thought when he heard him speak. And his manners were impeccable. His hands might be massive, but his fingernails were clean and manicured. Devin worked in a beauty salon. He always looked at the fingernails. Lionel chewed his. And the hands were so expressive. Devin had visions of them stroking his forearm—he'd wondered whether the blind date would be all over him. This wasn't at all what he expected. He almost wished . . .

"Where were you thinking of eating dinner?" Marcus asked.

"I hadn't thought," Devin answered. "Andre said you'd pick someplace." A steak house, Devin now wondered. He'd originally thought it probably would be McDonalds or KFC.

"I know of a Japanese restaurant that serves the best tempura. Sushi too, if that's your interest."

"Tempera would be fine," Devin said. More than fine.

Devin had taken a taxi to Tracks because Andre said Marcus had a car. It turned out not to be the pickup truck Devin expected. It was a Pontiac Solstice, a sleek sports car that was out of production—the whole company was out of business. But the Solstice was a collector's item now.

"How do you keep this honey on the road?" Devin asked, as he entered the car. The inside was impeccably clean. Devin doubted that a take-out meal had ever seen the inside of this vehicle.

"My family owned a Pontiac dealership too," Marcus said. "Kept enough parts for a Solstice to keep this one going. I worked there for years and can maintain the car myself."

When they both were in the car, Marcus looked over at Devin. Would he or wouldn't he, Devin wondered. They were finally alone alone; if a blind date was interested in anything at the end of the date, this, Devin thought, would be a time to signal that.

Marcus would, in a much more understated way than Devin thought might be the case when they were alone.

"Would you mind?" Marcus asked, leaning a bit into the passenger side of the car and putting an arm on the top of the seat behind Devin's head. "You are just so much more than I expected."

Devin leaned a bit in acceptance toward Marcus, who cupped his chin lightly and came in for a gentle kiss on the lips. "Umm, that was nice, sweet," he murmured. He lingered for a moment looking into Devin's eyes, his thumb tracing the curve of Devin's lower lip. Devin fought the urge to open his mouth and pull the thumb in.

But before that naturally could happen Marcus twisted back to face the windshield, pulled on driving gloves, and turned to concentrating on his driving. He drove fast and unexpectedly aggressively, but expertly. In total control. Devin felt totally safe in the man's hands.

The perfect gentleman, Devin thought. The signal the Devin got was that Marcus would continue to be the perfect gentleman—that he wasn't really all that interested in anything beyond having company for the evening, with just a hint of sensuality so that Devin wouldn't feel rejected. This was just going to be a companionable evening.

The football game was mostly business with Marcus. It's what he had come here for. Marcus was there for a purpose, but he also paid attention to Devin, explaining the intricacies of this and that. He didn't treat Devin like an idiot, though. He even took time to ask about the concerts and plays Devin went to—and didn't give a sour look when Devin mentioned opera and ballet. Their conversation at dinner had centered on the arts, and Marcus seemed to know as much about many aspects of that as Devin did.

After the game, they went back to Tracks for another drink and some dancing. A lot of the guys on the dance floor tried to cut in for Marcus' attention, but he politely waved them off and concentrated on Devin.

At the entrance to Devin's apartment building, when Devin assumed it would be another brief, sweet kiss, and the end of a tame, but surprising and interesting blind date, he was proved right about the kiss, but not about the rest.

Pulling away from a sweet, short kiss, Marcus looked Devin directly in the eye and said, "May I come in for a few minutes? Maybe a drink?"

"A few minutes? A drink?"

"Or maybe something more? I think you're really cute. And I think we hit it off fine. You know I'd like to . . . with you . . . to you."

"And?" Devin whispered.

"On you . . . in you. Inside you. I could take good care of you, baby. Don't you want to feel me inside you?" He looked like a little hopeful puppy dog. His voice, the smooth baritone, was so soft spoken that the words themselves—the unmistakable sexual intent of them—were muted. He had an arm behind Devin again, the fingers of that hand pressing into Devin's shoulder. And he was tracing Devin's lower lip lightly with a thumb of the other hand, having taken his driving glove off first.

Devin sighed. He had originally it would come to this—or strongly suspected it would, although he had been beginning to question that. Question it enough to maybe be slightly disappointed it might not become a choice, a possibility.

He leaned forward and they kissed sweetly again, with Devin pulling away just as Marcus' lips were pressing his to open and Devin felt the flicker of a tongue between his lips.

"You can come in . . . for a bit. We'll see."

"Is that a yes? I want to fuck you."

"That's a we'll see how it goes," Devin said, as he opened the passenger door and rolled out of the sports car. He still didn't know himself. It was a blind date, a first meeting. He was attracted—hell, more like aching for him, while still being scared of the size of him. But he didn't want to seem to be a pushover. The guy was cultured and sensitive. Surprisingly so. And he was big and black. It was new, possibly dangerous ground for Devin.

Devin was returning from his kitchen with two glasses of white wine—what they'd settled on that Devin could supply—and almost dropped the glasses.

Marcus was sitting on the sofa—naked. His clothes were neatly folded on a nearby chair, his polished boots lined up perfectly under the chair. A bigger shock than that he was naked was that he didn't really look naked. In his clothes he had looked clean cut. His nakedness revealed that his body was a riot of tattoo patterning and coloring on nearly every square inch of skin that had been covered by his clothes. He had suddenly transformed from a southern gentlemen—albeit a black one—to a primeval native. And there was no hiding that he was enormously erect or that there was a thick silver Prince Albert ring in the bulb of his cock.

His demeanor made the extraordinary change to the wild side as well.

"Come here, baby," he commanded, a harder edge to his voice than Devin had heard before.

In a trance, Devin put the wine glasses down on the dining room table he was standing beside, spilling both, his hands were trembling so badly. He took one tentative step toward the sofa, confused and in shock.

"I said come here," Marcus growled. "How did you think this fucking date was going to end? Been thinking of getting inside your sweet little ass since Andre showed me that nude photo of you."

Nude photo? What nude photo? No one but Lionel had nude photos of him. Without thinking, Devin had moved close enough for Marcus to reach out, grab him by the wrist, and pull him down on his knees between the black footballer's spread thighs. His cock was enormous. It didn't look exceptionally thick only because it was so long. And hard. It was only because it nearly dislocated Devin's jaw that he realized it was thick too.

Devin was made to deep throat it and hold, again and again, gagging and fighting for breath, while Marcus chanted "Take it, take it, take all of it" in a raspy growl. The thick PA ring in the cock head clicked against Devin's teeth until the bulb got to the back of his throat. Marcus held Devin's head between his massive hands like a vice and pulled his face on and off the cock again and again. Then Marcus was forcing Devin to deep throat and hold until Devin was gagging. Release, and then again. Pulling out after more than ten minutes of this, he creamed Devin's cheek and eyelids, up into the blond curl that kept falling over Devin's forehead. He came in for a brutal kiss and licked the cum off the still-shocked young man's face.

Marcus came up off the sofa, pulled Devin off his knees and quickly stripped him of his clothes. Devin, working his jaw to ensure that it wasn't unhinged, remained numb to what was happening to him and docile as the items were shed and thrown haphazardly to the side. How does a small twink like Devin fight off two-hundred pounds of black bruiser anyway?

Having gotten Devin naked and done a bit of groping and fondling—enough to have Devin, aware of what came next, moaning and whimpering, "Oh, God, be good to me; don't split me," Marcus slung him, belly down over the back of the sofa. Devin's arms and head hung defenselessly, uselessly in the face of the size and weight difference between the two, toward the floor. He moaned and groaned as Marcus spread his butt cheeks apart and ate his ass out, muttering "Open it, open it, open to me." Other than Marcus' mutterings in that deep baritone of his, all Devin could hear was the clicking of the metal clips against each other at the ends of Marcus' swaying dreadlocks.

Devin grunted and groaned as Marcus reached through his legs and grabbed his balls, rolling and squeezing them, and then roughly milked the young blond's cock while slapping and biting his buttocks, thumping his hole with his fingers, digging his fingers into and tonguing his hole deeply, Marcus sharply commanding throughout that Devin "Relax, open to me, baby. We're gonna do this; you're gonna take me. You're gonna take it big. You're gonna love every inch of it." Devin writhed and moaned under the onslaught.

How could Devin relax to this assault on his privates? How could he take that monster cock? But then, miraculously, as Marcus tongued the hole deep and his milking of Devin's cock became rhythmic, less rough, and after Devin had released his cream with a jerk and a sigh, Devin did feel himself sighing, relaxing his passage, and moving his hips back rhythmically to meet the dig of the tongue.

This didn't last too long until Marcus was satisfied that Devin would take him—something Devin would never have imagined he could do, but that he did. Devin felt the weight of the two-hundred-pound muscular athlete crouch over him close as he was draped over the back of the sofa, and he let out a deep, rumbling cry as, preceded by the thick PA, Marcus' cock split the difference between the curves of Devin's butt cheeks and started its long journey up his passage. Marcus reached down, grabbed a handful of blond, curly hair on the back of Devin's head and pulled it hard toward him, arching Devin's back to him.

The fuck started off with a deep pounding, built up from there to the music of Marcus' thrashing dreadlock clips and Devin's plaintive cries of "Fuck me, fuck me, fuck me," involuntarily pulled from him by the intensity of the attack and the depth of the digging cock, and only settled down into a rhythm of long, deep slides, after Devin was reduced to a whimpering rag doll under the relentless power of the big, black muscleman.

Half way through the fuck, Marcus latched the broad palm of one hand on one of Devin's pecs and grasped Devin's chin with the other one and held Devin tight into his muscular torso, Devin's cheek next to his, as he thrust up into Devin's channel, resuming the chant of "Take it, take it, take all of it" in Devin's ear. Devin dug his fingernails in the top edge of the sofa and held on for dear life.

Marcus took him hard, deep, swiftly, and at great length, while Devin moaned and whimpered, his begging for mercy turning into declarations of how totally he was being taken until it all subsided into gurgles and soft whimpering.

When Marcus filled out the bulb of his condom—Devin had long since come a second time—he remained plastered on Devin's back, running his hands over Devin's body and whispering what a cute little trick he was. About the time Devin thought that was all there was going to be to the assault, though, Marcus pulled away from him, slung Devin over his shoulder, and headed for the bedroom.

He put Devin on all fours on the bed, mounted him, and fucked him hard and fast to the music of his gyrating dreadlock clips to another ejaculation. As he felt the hard curve of the PA at his hole, reamed now to fit Marcus' requirements, Devin lowered his chest and cheek to the bedspread, presented his tail for a straight shot, widened the

42

spread of his legs, stretched one arm out to grab a fistful of material to steady himself, reached under his belly with his other hand to fist his own cock, and, with a whimper, surrendered all to his master. Gripping Devin's hips between strong hands, Marcus pounded, pounded, pounded away inside his young blond prey, rightfully claiming victory. Meeting no resistance; taking no prisoners.

"Ah, yeah, good, a perfect fit now," Marcus muttered as he pumped. "That gets it now, doesn't it?" He could—and no doubt did—take Devin's low, drawn-out moaning as agreement.

Devin was so worn out by the second fucking that he just collapsed on the bed, softly moaning. His head and an arm hung over one side of the bed where the thrustings of the black giant's cock had moved his battered body. As Marcus rose off him, the black bull slapped him hard on the rump and cheerily exclaimed, "That was a good workout. Good date. A sweet, tight ass. Great little body. Takes a little work, but the hole opens up enough. Andre told me you were a good lay; he sure was right about that." After that favorable and cheerful assessment of the evening's work, he sauntered off to the adjoining bathroom to help himself to a shower.

"Not tight anymore," Devin murmured, with a deep groan.

After he'd dressed, once more becoming the Virginia gentlemen, Marcus briefly visited the bedroom, leaning over Devin's prone and still-trembling body, ruffled Devin's curly blond locks affectionately, and gave him a tender, lingering kiss on the back of the neck. This time, when Marcus rubbed a thumb lightly over Devin's lower lip, Devin pulled the thumb into his mouth and sucked it for a few seconds. To the victor go the spoils.

Devin waited to hear the front door to the apartment click shut before he dragged his bruised body off the bed, struggled over to his desk, turned on the computer, and started to work the keys.

* * * *

"It's you," Devin said, as, rubbing the sleep out of his eyes the next morning, he answered the door. "I thought you still had a key."

"I do," Lionel said. "But I didn't think we were on that ground of familiarity anymore."

There was something in his voice, something smug, that had Devin look sharply at him before he turned and padded toward the coffee pot in the kitchen. Lionel entered the apartment and shut the door behind him. He looked around for evidence of what he expected to see. Yes, the sofa looked like it had done battle and lost. He could see through the door to the bedroom that there'd been a frantic skirmish in there too. Devin was a neatnic, definitely neater than this, when left to himself.

"So, you said you wanted to date other guys. How is that working for you?" He sat on the sofa and gave a good sniff. Yep, smelled like sweat, musk, and lust. He smiled a little smile.

Devin came out of the kitchen carrying two cups of coffee. Looking around at him, Lionel saw the two wine glasses on the dining table—and the liquid spill. He smiled into his cup as he lifted it to his mouth.

He also saw that Devin grimaced as he moved and wasn't walking straight. Andre had told him about Marcus Black and how he dated—that he was hung like a horse and had a powerhouse thrust. Lionel almost felt sorry for Devin, but not really. The little prick had dumped him. Well, the little prick had found out how rough it could get out in the dating world.

"I'm doing just fine," Devin said, giving Lionel a level stare. He'd worked it out in the middle of the night.

Marcus' connection to Andre. Andre's connect to Lionel. Lionel's pettiness—which was a big reason Devin left him—leaving him for that and because Lionel was a vanilla fucker. No excitement or testing with Lionel. Never had been. Never the feel of a breathtaking date. They might as well have been . . . married.

"In fact I had a date last night with a big black football player one and a half times my size and with a cock twice the size of yours. We had a great date and then he came home with me and fucked the stuffing out of me. I've been up for hours writing black bruiser on white twink fuck stories for an anthology for my publisher. I think he's going to love them."

"You're shitting me," Lionel said, setting his coffee cup down on the coffee table lest he spill it in his consternation. "You got banged hard by a black bull last night, and you aren't curled up in a fetal ball this morning?"

"Nope. Marcus is coming back to scout the Nighthawks' game next Saturday. We have a date to do it all over again. He agreed to stay the night this time and do me on the hour. He fucked me just the way I've been aching to be fucked. He really knows how to date a man."

It had been worth it—his little speech—to see the expression on Lionel's face. The most rewarding part was that it all was true. Marcus had called him on his cell from the Solstice fifteen minutes after he'd left, asking Devin for a follow-up date, and Devin had been quick as he could be to say yes

Clay and Jose

"And do you like colored men?"

Jose looked up at the guy sitting opposite him.

"I think I said that in my profile. Yes, I do like dark-skinned men."

"Dark as me?" Clay asked.

"Sure," Jose replied, looking across at the chocolate-colored twink sitting opposite.

"Was chocolate what you were expecting?" Clay asked.

Ouch, he is so insecure, Jose thought. Cute guy, but can I stand the neediness? "So, do you like animals?" he asked, instead of replying. Wondering if he should think of some reason to leave.

"Animals? Sure. I have a dog and a canary. You?"

"Oh. No, I share a flat and it's a no-pets building. What sort of dog?"

"A Masteen. It's a Galician, Spanish, sheepdog. Big. My uncle breeds them in Colorado. Best in the U.S."

"Oh. Gee . . ." Jose said, lost for words. "So, you have a big yard?"

"No, only small, but I run with him twice a day. I think I said that in my profile—that I run. A dark-skinned runner. You said you train and you look like you do. What sort of training?"

"I do triathlons. Bike, swim, run. Lots of training. It gets boring at times on my own. I was hoping to maybe find someone who also ran, but with a dog, it must be slower."

"Oh no, I have trouble keeping up with Masty at times, and I used to run cross-country in comps."

Jose was taking another look at the dark twink opposite him. He was not such an air head as a lot of those he arranged to meet were. He did like them to be twinks.

"So, triathlons. You work too?"

"No. I have a sports scholarship, so study and train. Just came off three months heavy training. On a break."

Clay was wondering how dim Jose was. He was sounding like he did nothing but train. "And dating colored men . . . how does that fit in? What is it about colored men that appeals to you?"

"Um. I like dating good-looking guys, any color," Jose admitted. "So, you like dating white guys?"

"Well, I wouldn't be here if I didn't, would I?" Clay replied. "I like that chocolate and vanilla thing. I like guys who like to see that too. I have a mirror over my bed and I like to watch myself doing it with a white guy. Particularly a fit one." He smiled at Jose. Jose's dick was unexpectedly getting hard. "So, do you like that look, chocolate and vanilla wound together, fucking? Black dick, white dick, white hole with a black dick working in it? I really like watching that," he added in a husky voice, his eyes fixed on Jose's.

"Ah. A mirror." Jose was trembling, thinking on the black dick in white hole bit. He was versatile but had expected to be the one pinning this chocolate twink. "So, you're top?" he stammered.

"I top, I bottom, but I wanna top you. Wanna see my black cock running into your white hole, making it big

47

and open. Running in and out, in and out. Seeing and hearing my black balls slapping your white ass when I go deep." His voice was dark and husky now, low and rumbling. A big sexy voice.

"OH." Clay's eyes were almost closed as he thought of it. His hand moving to his cock.

"I like to ride a guy on his knees until he falls to the bed. Like to ride a guy like he's a wheelbarrow—gives a great view of my cock in his hole. Me seeing it myself and in the mirror. A three-dimensional view of the fuck. So, Jose, do you want me to watch my black dick fuck you in 3D?" Clay said it leaning into Jose, his feet under the table doing things to Jose's legs and groin. "Chocolate and vanilla. Close up. A mirror. Wanna see it?"

"Erhhh, yeah sure," Jose stammered.

"So let's go." Clay said, leaping out of the café booth and bouncing on his toes, raring to go.

Jose eased himself out of the booth, breathing heavily, wanting to grab the twink and do him right there. See his white cock pumping Clay's twinky chocolate ass. Pounding it till he had made the twink cry for mercy. Turning him while he pumped, looking down at him as his eyes rolled up in his head and he begged for more white cock. Jose wrapped his arms around Clay and pulled him close, kissing him as he rubbed his hard dick against the twink's hard dick. Clay joining in, wriggling his butt and leaning in, planting his hands on Jose's butt. Squeezing his cheeks with strong fingers. Showing who was in control.

My First Black

June, 1974, Da Nang Airbase, Vietnam

God, he was big; one of the biggest. Shit, he could fuck. Panting, panting, I grabbed the metal legs of the cot on either side in a death grip, my cheek pressed into the rough woolen blanket, my eyes bugging out and my mouth slack and open in a silent scream, as he drove it harder, deeper inside me. Cruel. Rough. Just what I wanted. Just what I needed.

"Punish me," I uttered in a gritted-teeth effort not to scream it out. "Cum inside me."

He laughed.

My knees were trembling and I was about to collapse under the weight of the big black bull covering my back. Driving harder, deeper. For one long moment in time I no longer was in a half hut, half tent alongside the Da Nang airstrip. I was dancing on the clouds with the cock of a big black bull churning inside me. Far, far away from the periodic dull booms in the night, listening for the whistle of the rocket in flight, wondering if the next one would land on top of me—of us, before he could blast up into my stomach.

"Hurry. Now! Hurry. Give it to me, give it to me. Give me your cum," I gasped, daring not to yell it out as I wished to do because of the close proximity of the other huts. I threw both of my hands back to grasp his undulating buttocks and to press him close into me as he went rigid, muttered, "Oh shit, man, I'm coming," and then, with a series of jerks, did, creaming my passage deep.

He came off me and I rolled out from under him, both of us going sideways on the cot, our feet on the dirt floor, and our shoulder blades leaning into the rough wood of the huts lower walls. We didn't say anything yet. He was finished; I wasn't. He half turned to me, placing the heel of a hand under my balls, with two fingers in my channel, finger fucking me as I jacked off my cock. If it had been Willy, we would have kissed at this point, while I was taking care of myself. But the sergeant, older than I was by a good six years, and all rank conscious except in the heat of it, when he aroused me with his race domination, was all business, all cruel domination when he fucked me. Of the two, though, he had the more solid body, and, although they were both horse hung, the thicker cock and the greater control.

He also punished me as I needed to be punished— for what I was.

There were times, like this, that I preferred Mel. The older man was more experienced and more in control. Whereas Willy could take me to the heights quicker and higher, Mel could make me dance on the clouds—and forget about where I was—longer. These days in Nam, the longer I could have my mind on somewhere else, the better. And he could put me firmly in my place.

When I'd shot my load, in an arc over onto the floor beyond my knees, we both gave a deep sigh. Mel reached over to the table at the bottom of the cot and rolled two joints, lighting both in his mouth, and then handing one to me.

"That was a quick one," he said. He was fisting his black, monster cock, which was showing signs that it wasn't satisfied for the night.

"We have time for another," I answered. "We were both keyed up. The rocketing has picked up. And it's coming too close."

"How long you expect we can hold out here, Lieutenant?"

"Haven't you heard, Sergeant? We're winning the war."

We both laughed. Watching him stroke his cock was driving me crazy. I fisted mine and languidly pulled on it as I took another drag on the joint. We both were naked from the waist down but still in our khaki athletic Ts. If it had been Willy, I'd have had his T off and would be sucking on his nipples now, and I'd be the one with a fist on his cock, ready, willing, and able to do it again. Willy was a young private, virile, always hard, always ready to go again. Proud of his nine incher and always ready to spike me. And passionate, a real lover. Even Willy knew there was a difference and reveled in it when he fucked me—him no longer the private and me the lieutenant.

Mel did it to get his rocks off and, like me, to push the war out of his mind for the seconds he was releasing his load—and to show me who bested who.

He saw me eying his shaft. "Quite a snake, ain't it?" he asked. "An anaconda."

"Yes it is. You're a man among men. I loved every inch of it."

"Eight and a half. Willy's longer, but I'm thicker."

"Yes, yes you are."

"You know any white man or Gook here who is longer or thicker?"

"No, no I don't."

"You fucked by any white men at all? All I know you go under is Willy and me."

"Yes, just you and Willy."

"Is it because we're the biggest or because we're black?"

I didn't answer for the longest minute. "I think it's because you're black," I finally said.

"Most white men wouldn't be caught dead under a black man, let alone let a black man do what I do to you."

"Yes, I think that's true—still."

"They don't know what they're missing."

"No, no, they don't."

"Willy or me your first black man?"

"No. My first was a good ten years ago, the summer of '64. Birmingham, Alabama."

Mel whistled. "You ran some sort of risk going under a black boy in Birmingham in those days."

"Yes, we risked it all," I answered, my mind going back to then and to my first black lover. It was on a blind date. It was going so well, once I was into it, and almost ended up so bad.

"Preferring going under black men have anything to with Birmingham in the summer of '64?"

"Yeah, maybe so. My form of protest—and of penance."

"Well, Mr. White Lieutenant, get down on your knees and suck this black sergeant's snake. Then I'll fuck you long and slow—and deep and hard and fast. But, no, white boy, better yet, you'll fuck yourself on it."

"God, yes," I whispered.

I sank between his spread thighs and took his thick, thick cock inside my mouth. When he was as big as I could take him—bigger than that, it seemed at the time—I came up into his lap, and sank as far as I could down on the cock, facing away from him, with my hands planted on his knees, because I knew Mel didn't want the intimacy, whereas Willy would want to do it face to face. With Mel palming my pecs in those big black hands of his, I fucked myself on his rod, sobbing at the thickness of it and sinking lower and lower on it until I could feel the coarse short hairs of his pubes scratching on my buttocks. As I bottomed on him, with a whistling roar of a rocket coming in almost too close overhead, the two of us exploded together.

"Get off my prick, whitey," Mel growled when we'd come together. He roughly pushed me off to the side. We both knew it was because I wanted that level of submission. By the time he'd pulled his shorts on and reached the door, he was back in military form, turning and saluting and saying, "I'll get the KP roster to you tomorrow morning, sir."

* * * *

Summer, 1964, Birmingham, Alabama

I hadn't known it was going to be a date, blind or otherwise. I certainly didn't know it would turn out as it did.

Nelson rolled off between my legs, where he'd just deposited a load inside my ass, quickly pulled on his jeans, and went over to the door and unlocked it. We couldn't go very long behind locked doors in this old motel, opened again just to accommodate the protestors from up north, or everybody would know what was going on in the room.

He plopped down in a wobbly straight chair and turned his eyes on me. I was still finishing myself, stroking my cock, legs still bent and spread from where Nelson had been lying between them.

"Put that away," he said. "Anyone could walk in here."

"You didn't finish me, so . . . ah, here it comes." And it did. I came, reached over the side of the bed to retrieve my T-shirt, used it to wipe myself off, and then reached over for my jeans. That's all either one of us was wearing. It was a hot, hot, hot August in Birmingham.

Nelson, a sunny blond, had an athletic build. I was slimmer, but I was well-muscled too from having been on the high school swim team. That's where we'd met—on the swim team at Jeb Stuart High School in Northern Virginia, although Nelson had been on the football team too, which accounted for his well-defined musculature.

He was always the dominant one. He was a senior, a standout jock, when I was a sophomore. I worshipped him. We were on the swim team together just that one year. But that was enough. He also was the rich one. He lived in the exclusive Lake Barcroft section; his father owned a string of bowling alleys across the Virginia and Maryland suburbs of D.C. The subdevelopment I lived in was nice enough, but military officers didn't make great salaries then, so we spent more time at his house, which had a dock on the lake so we could both boat and swim in good weather. The money difference also meant he went to Penn State, where he'd made the varsity football team already, and I was enrolled at the University of Virginia the next year. It was just as good a school at Penn State, but, with in-state tuition, at a fourth of the price.

We'd been fucking for two months, ever since just before I'd graduated from Jeb Stuart and not long before he convinced me to go with him on a protest trip down to Alabama, which was the "cool" thing for northern upper-middle-class white college students to do at the time. I pushed tradition in being released from high school and being eighteen. I'd fucked my prom date in the backseat of my dad's car and then gone bowling with Nelson, and he'd fucked me behind the mechanical pin setters, with pins bouncing around in front of us and the noise of the falling pins covering my cries of being taken as I leaned into the back of one of the machines and he fucked me from behind. I found I preferred Nelson's cock to my prom date's cunt, not that she wasn't willing and begging for it.

Everyone with money and a conscience—all white, of course—who was also young was going down to the deep south that summer to join in the civil rights protests. It was what would make men of us, Nelson had said.

I thought that Nelson fucking me was what had made men of us, but Nelson wanted me to go with him, so I did, both of us taking off in his new Buick Skylark convertible. I thought that name was prophetic as I saw this trip just as a "life's button" lark that Nelson had to punch. I didn't think about the danger of it at all. Truth be known, I didn't think much about it being to establish rights for blacks, either. I'd met a few blacks, but there were none in my life, school, church, or community. Nelson's family did have a black maid, though, and as far as I could see, Mamie was more of a mother to him than either one of his parents were.

Maybe that's what motivated Nelson to want to come down to Birmingham—or maybe it was just that it was what all white college students were doing—to protest more than just the suppression of blacks.

"We're giving a couple of guys rides to the concert tonight and there's a party of the workers afterward—to celebrate our last day down here."

"Fine," I said. And so that's where the double blind date started coming into the picture. There was a Peter, Paul, and Mary concert in downtown Birmingham to celebrate what had been a couple of weeks of protests that everyone thought were having a favorable effect in breaking the back of the white backlash in the deep south to new federal laws. The group of civil rights workers we'd come down with from the Mid-Atlantic states was going back home—all of us with colleges to get to. There was only a smattering of cars among the workers, with Nelson's being among the snazziest ones. I assumed we were giving rides to a couple of the white workers—all of those in our group were white and upper middle class. I was wrong.

"This is LeRoy and this is Clem," Nelson said, cutting through my shock that the pair he was giving rides to were black. One of them, LeRoy, a senior at Alabama A&M in Huntsville, was an ebony god, rich dark chocolate in complexion and just as handsome and muscular and chip-on-his-shoulder as he could be. The other, Clem, was a drifter, picking up work here and there, he said. A lot of seasonal harvesting work. He was tall and gangling and a much lighter chocolate than LeRoy was.

There were the four of us, separate, and a bit awkward with each other during the Peter, Paul, and Mary concert. Neither Nelson nor I had come into direct, individual contact with black men before, even though we were down here putting up a line of solidarity with them. We had marched, but even in the marches in those days in Birmingham, you could see a race divide in all but the spearhead group along the parade line.

By the party afterward, where there was booze and dancing and everyone was letting their hair down and their steam out at the end of a dangerous and nerve-wracking protest season, there was no divide between whites and blacks. The four of us drifted into being naturally paired up. LeRoy was with Nelson—heavily with Nelson, the two of them dancing close, drinking hard, and eyeing each other with intent. That left Clem with me. Somehow Clem had been apprised that Nelson fucked me, because he was getting friendly and frisky with his hands during the party. I, on the other hand, was tensing up. I knew I should relax and just hang, but this was all new and disconcerting to me. I didn't really know how to act around blacks. Despite everything I wanted to believe, they scared me a bit. And, other than Nelson, I didn't know what to do when a man wanted to put his hands on me, either.

We were partying in an old, abandoned plantation house, which was the best that we could book in a Birmingham that didn't want us there in the first place. There were a couple of groups of young, white thugs moving about the grounds, hurling insults at the house and making verbal threats. But we were in too great a strength in the house for them to do more than that. They'd probably also heard that we were clearing out the next day. Standing up for principles didn't cut it when we had to appear for classes the next week.

When we left the party, Nelson drove only partway down the road leading out to the main highway. He turned off on a track leading into a stand of trees and turned the car off. He and LeRoy were in a clutch immediately. Clem put an arm around me in the backseat as well, and I stiffened. I gave a little moan, though, when he pulled me into him, one hand on the back of my head, guiding my face to his for a kiss, and moved the other hand to my basket. He was rubbing me through the material of the jeans and I couldn't help but harden for him.

In the front seat, LeRoy already had at least his shirt off in the passenger seat and Nelson was in his lap, facing him, and pulling his shirt over his head. The shirt off, he lowered his face to LeRoy's for a deep kiss.

I covered Clem's invasive hand and moved it away from my basket.

"You're hard for me," he said, pulling away from the kiss momentarily and gave a low, guttural laugh.

I couldn't deny it, but I could try to ignore that he had pointed it out.

I tried to give him nothing in the kiss too, but he pressed his tongue between my lips and I slowly gave way to him. The kiss became a lot more sensual and possessive. His body moved more over mine, signaling he was taking possession of me. I went with it; I couldn't help myself from doing so. He kissed so much better than Nelson did.

Clem took my hand again and guided it to where I could tell he wanted me to touch flesh. He had his cock out.

"Touch it," he murmured, as he broke from the kiss. "I've got nine inches for you when it's hard. Make it hard."

"No." It came out in a low gasp. "I can't. We shouldn't."

"We can; we should. You came down here to empower the blacks. I'll show you what power is."

"Nooo," I moaned. But he'd put my hand on his cock, which was hardening. My fingers involuntary closed around it. He groaned at the small victory.

"Your other hand too," he commanded. "you can't handle it all even with two hands. Think of it all inside you." He took my other hand and made me grasp the cock above the handhold I had at the root of it. Sure enough, even with both hands, one above the other, I didn't reach the bulb.

I began to tremble almost uncontrollably. I looked into the front seat, where Nelson obviously was on LeRoy's cock, rising and falling on it, and they were doing a lip lock.

Clem took my mouth again in a deep kiss, and I felt him unbuckling and unzipping my jeans and pulling them off my legs.

No, no, don't. I might have thought I said it, but if I did, he paid me no heed. He was nearly on top of me, his head over mine, his face turned down to mine, a thigh over mine, pinning them to the seat. It was a position of control, and my body knew it and relaxed to it. He was going to fuck me. He knew it; my body knew it. I'd never been fucked by a black man before; I'd never been fucked by a nine-inch cock before.

But that was going to happen now.

He had a grasp on my cock, which was hardening for him, and he was stroking it. I had only one hand on his cock, but I found myself stroking it to the same rhythm he was doing with mine. His was lengthening and hardening. Throbbing to my touch. He was going to have me.

He pulled his mouth away from mine. "Suck it. Suck my cock," he demanded.

"Please. I don't—"

"What's the matter? This a game you're playing, coming down here to support my people, but my cock isn't good enough for whitey to suck?" He moved away from me, and using the hand cupping the back of my head, he pulled my face down to his lap. I moaned, but didn't resist him. And then I had his cock inside my mouth, sucking it and gagging on it as the bulb hit the back of my throat. It wasn't thick but it was the longest cock I'd ever seen. I'd gotten some good looks in locker rooms, but nothing compared with this.

Guiding my head with one broad-palmed hand, he let the other glide down my back, over my T-shirt, onto the flesh of my naked buttocks, and into my crack. He was able to reach my hole, and, with a long finger, he entered me, moving the finger in and out, teasing me to open to him, which I did.

Nine inches. Nine inches. I knew I'd really have to open to him.

"Relax it. Open it to me," he muttered. A second finger went in and then a third. Remembering what I did for Nelson's cock as it entered me, I let my ass muscles relax.

"Good. Nice," he murmured.

The moon was out full, and I became aroused at the contrast in the hues of our skin. Although Clem's body was a light chocolate brown and the palms of his hands and soles of his now-unsandaled feet were as light as my skin, his cock was jet black. I shuddered at the up-close aspect of a jet-black shaft. I'd given Nelson blow jobs. I wasn't above that. And what I was feeling now was so much more sensual than anything with Nelson.

59

Now that I was into it with Clem, I treated his cock right—luxuriating in being able to suck it and grasp it with a fist at the same time. Rubbing the shiny blackness of it. The bulb was big and long, a pink color in stark contrast to the cock, and I played at pushing the foreskin of it down and then pulling it up, listening to him moan. I played with it as I let my fingers run down the thick veins of the silky black shaft. I opened my lips down to the rim of the bulb and sucked on like it was a lollypop. When I flicked my tongue on the piss slit, he lay back against the seat, his head thrown back, and groaned. "Yes, yes, just like that. You're good for a whitey, real good. Been teasin' me about not wantin' it."

Then, with a "Oh, shit, no more. You're gonna make me come," he was pulling out of my mouth, turning us, and pushing me down in the corner of the backseat. I no longer could see either Nelson or LeRoy above the top of the front seat, but the car was bouncing on its springs and the front seat was shimmering, so I guessed that LeRoy was on top of Nelson stretched between the two bucket seats up there and going to town inside him. Nelson had told me he went both ways. I guess this showed that he sure did. He was mouthing off something fierce about the size and attack of LeRoy. He cried out about coming and then all went still up there—but just for a minute or so before the rocking of the front seat started up again and Nelson was claiming he was being split apart.

What was going on in the front seat certainly wasn't tamping down my response to what was happening in the backseat. I had been prepared for the inevitability of being fucked. Now that Clem was getting around to it, I just lay there and let him have whatever he wanted.

Clem grabbed both of my ankles, wishboned my legs, raising them, and dipped his head down to where he, first, swallowed my cock and then my balls, and then was eating out my ass. I lay there, immobile and hyperventilating and moaned as he prepared me for nine inches, as I knew he was doing. All I could think of was that nine inches he had boasted he had.

And then they were inside me. He fed them into me slowly, but he gave them all to me. Clem hunched over me, right leg trapped high on the backseat cushion by his shoulder and my left ankle on his right shoulder, as he came in for the kill—entering, entering, entering me, as I writhed under him, trying, unsuccessfully, halfheartedly, ineffectually to pull away from his possessing lips, and moaned the invasion of the longest cock I could ever think of taking. When he began to pump, I tore my lips away from his, arched my head back over the side of the car, and cried out, "Oh, God. Oh, shit. FUCK ME!"

He compiled, but only for five or six minutes before coming inside me and collapsing on top of me, both of us panting hard.

In the front seat, a divinely muscular and naked LeRoy was sitting on the seat back on his bulbous and hard-muscled buttocks, his legs draped over Nelson's shoulders, his hands holding Nelson's head, as Nelson deep throated him.

"It'll be better out of the car," Clem murmured. "In a few, we'll go out under the trees and do it right."

Do it right? Do it again? With Nelson, who had never fucked me like that, it was one and done. This black master with a fire hose for cock was going to fuck me again? I moaned deeply, and he gave me a low laugh. I wondered how soon "again" was, but that was answered immediately—and wasn't going to happen out of the car. He was hardening again. And he was pumping again. Nearly ten minutes this time, and I had already come up his belly, when he released his seed a second time.

"That was nice. Your ass is sweet." Clem had whispered that. I didn't have the breath to say anything.

Nelson and LeRoy were moving into the backseat when, grabbing a lap robe, Clem was pushing me out of the car and guiding me further down the track to a mossy patch between the gnarled roots of a large oak tree.

Given the expansion of room, we sixty-nined on the blanket, rolling around to where he was on top, then I was on top, and then we were side by side in a tight ball, me unsuccessfully trying to deep throat his cock alternating with sucking his balls, and Clem eating my ass out.

All inhibitions gone with the wind. I couldn't get enough of him now.

Young and virile and black, Clem fucked me twice more under the tree, coming in prodigious explosions each time and leaving my channel awash with cum that dripped down my thighs. The first time was athletic, with him standing and fucking me in a modified missionary, with my torso drifting down to the ground and my palms on the moist earth. Then, after a brief respite of kissing and cooing, he put me on all fours, covered and mounted me, and rode me hard.

This fuck wasn't actually completed, because just as he was shooting, he was being pulled, cursing and screaming, off me and rough hands were pulling me up and away from him.

"What do we have here?" A young white guy, one of five surrounding us, two holding me and three holding down Clem, said in a sneery voice. "Is this a rape of a white guy by a nigger? This is a tree-swing offense."

The other four allowed as it was, and while two of the thugs held me, writhing and cursing, between them, the other three gave Clem a beat down. I think they would have killed him—and certainly think they intended to—if LeRoy and Nelson hadn't heard them, turned the headlights of the car on, which got the thugs' attention real fast, and moved, yelling like a whole military unit, toward us.

The thugs let loose of Clem and me and melted into the trees.

"Into the car," Nelson commanded in a breathless voice.

"I think he needs a hospital," LeRoy said, as he knelt over Clem's body.

Hours later, after a trip to the hospital to leave off Clem, who they'd only need to keep overnight, the other three of us, relieved, were in LeRoy's room over a barbershop in the black section of Birmingham.

Nelson was sitting off to the side on a straight chair, stroking his cock and waiting his turn again—with LeRoy or me, I didn't know. We'd already gone through several permutations.

The dark chocolate god, LeRoy, was bent over me, looking deep into my eyes. His knees were pressed up under my buttocks, raising my pelvis to him, his fists buried in the mattress at either side of my shoulders. My hands were grasping his buttocks, holding him into me. I was gasping with the deep reach of each of the thrusts of the longest, thickest, jet-black cock I possibly would ever take—although I would certainly search far and wide and compare the thickness, reach, and strength of thrust of black cocks. He had been fucking me for ten minutes. I had no doubt he could go for thirty more if he wanted to. I was fully open to him to do whatever he wanted—and he obviously wanted it all, just like any other man of any color did.

As if sensing I had totally surrendered to him, LeRoy started pistoning me harder, faster, deeper. I let my head loll over to the side, whispering, "Yes, give it all to me. Cum inside me. Fill me with your black seed. I am your slave."

I was destined to search them out from then on, service them, and let them do whatever they wanted with me as punishment and penance for being white.

Tight Squeeze

We were squeezed in close together in a booth in the shadows of the noisy, smoke-fogged bar. This wasn't really my kind of place, but Chris had suggested it as a place to meet for our first look at each other. At least it was conveniently located in the same block as my office building. We had conversed for some time on a chat line and had become more explicit in maybe hooking up when we discovered we lived near the same city. I had honed in on him because he said he was in his early twenties and preferred more experienced men in their thirties who were still in good condition and were interested in topping younger men. That pretty much defined me. I got really interested when he said he'd been drawn to my profile because I had listed myself as eight inches. I had lied in that; I actually was eight and half inches, but if I'd told the truth few would have believed my claim. And then I was hooked when he revealed that he was mildly interested in bondage.

So, here we were, scoping each other out in person. He proved to be a lithe, but well-muscled and model-handsome blond with rather nervous mannerisms. He was wearing a designer T-shirt and low-slung worn jeans and looked very much the early twenties that he had claimed to be. I was wearing brown, casual pants, a close-fitting off-white dress shirt, and a camel-tan jacket with leather elbows, and I could tell that he was pleased with what he saw when he was first guided to the table.

We engaged in small talk for a bit while we waited for a waiter, with me creeping ever closer to him along the vinyl bench. I was up close to him, with my arm around him and my fingers stroking one of his nipples through his shirt when he zeroed in on the question of whether I really was eight inches. When I told him the truth, I could feel him trembling under the palm of my hand. He expressed disbelief, and I gave him permission to find out himself, right then and there. His hand went to my fly below the table surface, and he lowered the zipper to my pants and rolled out my hose. I could hear the intake of breath and feel his tremors increase as he found out that I had told the truth.

The waiter appeared, a pert young man, short of stature, but very well built and with freckles and golden-red hair that would have hung to his shoulders if he didn't have it tied up in a pony tail. He could tell in an instant what Chris and I had going on under the table top, but this was that kind of bar, so he just gave me a shy little grin as he took our orders. Chris ordered a domestic draft beer, and I ordered a martini.

As soon as the waiter disappeared, Chris sank under the table and had the head of my dick between his lips. He ran his tongue around my glans, at the rim and pushed at my piss slit with the tip of his tongue. After a bit of this, with my cock responding by beginning to harden, he took in about four inches of me and squeezed his mouth tight over my rod. It was time for me to show him what I expected. I wrapped my legs around his back tightly and grabbed his head on both sides with my hands. I held him close there, guiding his mouth up and down, and ever deeper on my cock, which had sprung to life when I had taken control. This tight closeness was what I liked, what I responded to sexually.

The waiter returned with our drinks and didn't seem at all surprised not to see Chris sitting beside me. I could tell he wasn't fooled into thinking that Chris was off in the men's room either. He took a little longer than normal in setting our drinks down and gave me that shy little smile again while I was busy face-fucking Chris under the table and trying to keep a straight face myself. The waiter turned and left, and I swear that I thought he twitched his bulbous butt at me while he walked off.

Despite some gurgling and gagging, Chris sucked me off quite expertly, licked my cock clean, and rolled my long dick back into my fly and zipped me back up before he reappeared at my side. He was grinning, and his eyes sparkled. He took a swig of beer and then turned to me. His hand went to my stomach, where he pulled my shirt up out of my pants and laid his palm gently on my flat belly. My arm went around his shoulders closely again and my fingers returned to tracing his now-very-erect nipple through his T-shirt.

"Man oh man, that was great," he said. "You are all that your e-mails promised."

"Is that it then?" I asked. "Have you had enough, or do you want all of that up your ass as well?"

"Yes, oh yes, please. I've taken it deep before. No problem."

I wondered if he would think it had been no problem when I'd done to him what I planned to do.

"So, should we set a date for that?" I asked.

"Today. Now," he responded, becoming all trembly, like an excitable thoroughbred racehorse. "Well, not right here, of course. But somewhere more convenient. One of the stalls in the men's . . ."

"I prefer more privacy," I said, moving my free hand to his basket and tracing his straining cock through his tight

66

jeans. He moaned for me in appreciation at the attention. "And a form of . . . mild confinement. You'd indicated that appealed to you. Were you telling the truth about that?"

"Yes, oh yes," Chris said, and he was licking his trembling lips with a sense of danger and excitement. My hand left his nipple and gently took the side of his head and guided his lips to mine. We kissed in something that started sweet and ended somewhat more brutal and insistent, with me asserting total control, my fingers digging into his hair and cheek, and him becoming submissive. He gasped when I freed his lips.

"My office has a transient apartment in a building on this block, and I have a key to it." I said. "If you really are serious about moving this to a new level, we could be there within a few minutes."

"Oh, yes, yes, please," Chris, said in a gaspy voice. And then he grabbed his beer, downing it, and rose, ready to leave.

I threw more than enough money on the table top for the drinks and the tip and scooted out of the bench. Our waiter was leaning over a table whispering something in the ear of a patron as we passed him on our way out, and I copped a feel of his nice rounded ass. He looked up and gave me a sensuous grin and a laugh.

Chris was quiet as he walked down the block and into the lobby of one of the high-rise apartment buildings that was next to my office building. I could feel him trembling at my side though as the elevator rose into the clouds. As soon as we entered the apartment, I slammed the door behind us, flipped on the lights, and spun Chris around and against the wall next to the door. I shrugged my jacket off onto the floor and in one swift move, pulled his T up and off him and threw that in back of me as well. We kissed wildly, as we both struggled with belt buckles and zippers and pulling pants and briefs off. While I kissed and nipped my way down his neck and around his nipples,

Chris unbuttoned my shirt. Before he could pull my shirt off my back, though, I slammed my chest and thighs against his, close. Close, like I liked it. I was more muscular than he was everywhere and had little trouble gaining control. We'd made quite clear in our e-mails that I was a top and he was a bottom. I pushed my cock between his thighs, right under his balls, and he opened the stance of his legs, thinking that was what I wanted, but I pulled in my legs close to the side of his and held his legs close together, with my cock held tightly between his legs. His cock, which rose up my belly between us, was engorging and bobbing back and forth, trying to break free. But I wouldn't let it. His hands were fluttering about me, trying to find a way to meet my advances with responses of his own, but I grabbed him by the wrists and held his hand high over his head. I slammed my forehead against his, our noses tip-to-tip, and our eyes staring directly into each other. Neither of us said a thing, but I held him there, staring him down, until I felt all of the tension and struggle draining out of him, giving me total control.

And then I dry humped him, fucking his tender inner thighs, as my cock got thicker and longer. His trembling increased, the nervous racehorse. We kissed, and in that he showed that I was in full control; his lips opened to mine and his tongue responded to mine, but he let me take the lead, the aggressive movements were all mine.

When he was completely submissive, I broke away and guided him into the bedroom. I laid him down in the center of the bed on his belly and opened a suitcase I had placed there earlier and took out the leather restraints. Chris trembled all over but said nothing as I cuffed his hands and tied them off together with a leather rope at the center of the strong brass headboard.

Then I spread his legs, pulled his cock between his legs and stroked him off with one hand while I tongued his asshole, getting it ready for me. He became more active then, stroking his cock into my hand and wiggling his butt in response to my tonguing, and I let him do that until he had cum in my hand. I went into the bathroom and wet a washcloth and cleaned his dick and the bedspread off. Then I went to the suitcase and got a condom packet and tube of lubricant and of hand lotion. I opened the packet and rolled the condom onto my dick. It only covered about half of my length. I then lathered up my dick with the lubricant and plopped a gob of it at his asshole.

Chris had been watching me, and he had tensed up tightly when he felt the lubricant at his hole. I took up the hand lotion tube, squeezed out a good amount and crouched astride his thighs. Starting with his neck and shoulders and biceps, I massaged his muscles, working out his tensions. I ran my hands around to his chest and massaged his pecs and nipples and down his abs. Then I did his back muscles and down to the small of his back. I moved farther down his body, next to his calves, with knees, and massaged his thighs and then up on his butt cheeks. He was slim-hipped; there were deep hollows at the sides of his butt cheeks, and his buttocks were two pert little mounds. I was a little worried whether he could take me at all, let alone the way I planned to fuck him.

The massage had released his tension, and he was quite calm now; the trembling had stopped and he was sighing in appreciation of the unexpected massage. I'm sure he had expected me to take him quickly and brutally. That wasn't quite my plan, however. My fingers went to his asshole, and I started to work the lubricant into his ass. He was tensing up a bit now, but I took it slowly, and he quieted down before I moved to a deeper level or added another finger. Soon I had two fingers from each hand in him and was finding that he indeed had been plowed before by big tools. I took the two hands and pulled in opposite directions, opening his hole to me. The sheathed head of my thunderous cock went to the opening, and he tensed

69

and gave a little lurch as he felt my long-anticipated cock at his door. I kept the fingers there, pushing my cock head between them and was in up to the rim of my dick head. Chris was panting and had arched his butt up and widened his legs to accommodate me. This was OK for now, but this wasn't my plan. I'd give him this, though, to help him adjust to the initial embedding of my sausage.

I pushed in another inch and held, while he moaned and grunted and panted. When his ass walls had adjusted to this, I slid in a couple of more inches while I slowly extracted my fingers. His butt came up even more and his back arched down. He let breathe that he must have been holding since I first entered him slowly escape and I could feel him calming down. He thought this was it. He thought the entry was the toughest part and that I'd just slowly glide up to the center of him as his ass adjusted to me.

It was time for some reality. I needed control and tightness for my own pleasure to spin out. I pulled out of him and rose off the bed. Chris looked around in surprise. He was talking to me, but I wasn't listening to him. I was consumed by my own urges and needs now.

I went back to the suitcase and extracted a couple of more leather belts and a pair of black gloves. I pulled Chris's legs together and wrapped the smaller of the belts around his ankles, holding them tightly together. The larger of the belts I wrapped around his calves just below his knees. His legs were encased now, held closely together. Just the way I liked them. I pulled the black gloves on and tested them by touch the index finger of my right hand to Chris's calf. He lurched as the low-level electrical shock, set at just a slight tad above tingle hit him. The shock would be activated at the tips of all fingers when the index finger was pressed to a surface.

Chris was making questioning noises again, as I straddled his thighs once more and repeated the massage I had given him earlier, starting with the shoulders and

70

biceps, but this time with ten points of low-level electrical shock. He didn't like it at all at first, but eventually, when he became assured that the shock wasn't going to go much above a tingling sensation, he gave into the pleasure of the experience. I worked my way down his back and across his butt cheeks. And then I draped myself along his side and entered his ass with the middle finger of one hand and pressed my index finger at the base of his cock under his balls. He practically lifted up off the bed at the sensations this created. I worked my other hand under his belly and got three fingers on the sides of his cock and the thumb and little finger on his balls. He babbled and writhed and grunted and groaned as the middle finger of my right hand pushed in until it rested on his prostate and other fingers of that hand went to his balls. He came in a gush a cum that I'm sure he'd never managed before and lay there limply, as I extricated myself and positioned myself on top of him for the main event.

I was crouched over him with my knees nudging in on his thighs again. I positioned my cock at his now-scrunched-together asshole and worked the head into the tight hole. I spread the palms of my hands on his butt cheeks and pulled them apart while I pushed my engorged ram in a couple of now-hard-fought inches, the pads of my fingers giving little shocks to Chris's tender flesh. He was crying out in pleasured pain and grunting at the now very tight intrusion.

I needed closeness and tightness now. I pushed a couple of more inches into his constricted ass canal, as my body took full possession of his. My legs pulled in closely, encasing his bound legs; my heaving belly dug into the small of his back; my chest pushed into his shoulders and my nipples brushed back and forth on his back. My arms wrapped around his torso, their shocking fingers surrounding and playing with his nipples; my chin hooked into his shoulder, and my lips, teeth, and tongue went to a

71

tender spot in his neck. And I squeezed his body hard with mine, as my throbbing hose unwound slowly up his constricted ass canal. Five inches. Six inches. Chris was crying for mercy. Seven inches. Chris was crying out in ecstasy. Eight inches and he was just laying there, limp. And then I started to stroke in and out, close friction of a thick eight and half-inch cock in a tight ass passage. This is the way I liked it. I could cum big this way. And, at length, I did.

After I was finished fucking Chris, I reached up and down and released his restraints. Then I stripped off the gloves and threw them to the side. But I just lay there, my dong eight and a half inches up Chris's ass and my arms and legs closely enclosing his, for a half hour or more. Chris lay quietly within my grasp, his breath becoming more and more regular. He probably was fearful of what I'd do if he started to move away from me. When I'd begun to cramp, I left him and went into the bathroom to shower off.

Remorse and embarrassment flooded into me as I stood under the shower, letting the cool water sluice the musk of deep sex off me. I was sure Chris would be gone when I returned. I tried to remember the content of my e-mail exchanges with him, searching for evidence that I had gone beyond the bounds we had previously discussed. I liked Chris—and he had submitted to me totally. I was ashamed that I might have hurt him or taken him beyond the limits of his expectations. I know that I had caused him physical pain. But from what I could tell, this was part of the thrill of being an S&M bottom. Perhaps most of all, he had turned me on. He had met my needs. I was afraid I'd gone too far and that maybe neither he nor anyone else could meet my needs without being harmed themselves.

As these thoughts were eating me and water was sluicing down my body and into the shower drain, the shower stall door was thrust open, and there Chris stood, still naked from the earlier sex.

Oh, no, I thought. We're going to have a confrontation, and here I am, wet and trapped in this shower.

"That was great! I've never felt a dick as fully in me before," he exclaimed. He brought his hands around from his back. He held the leather restraints in one hand and a condom packet and the lubricant tube in the other. "Can you do me again? Are you recharged enough yet?"

Surprise, surprise. My worry was for naught.

I exited the shower, and Chris rubbed me off with a towel, paying extra attention to my cock and balls. Then he opened the condom packet and rolled the sheath onto my engorging cock and lubed me down. He headed back toward the bedroom, but I took his arm and kept him in the bathroom. I put his hands back into the restraints and led him over to the toilet. Making him kneel on the toilet lid, I tied his hands up to a towel rack above the toilet. Then I tied off his ankles, so he wouldn't instinctively try to widen his leg stance while I was fucking him. I couldn't maximize my pleasure without his ass being tight. I then lubed up the fingers of one hand, and standing behind him above the toilet seat, I lubed his asshole. During this process, I fanned the palm of the other hand on his belly and leaned over and nuzzled the crook of his neck with my lips. He turned his head toward mine and we kissed deeply, as my lubed fingers found his prostate and my other hand moved to stroking his cock and rolling and squeezing his balls.

I stroked his cock until he came, and then I moved in, covering him with my body, my legs pressing his thighs together and my arms wrapped around his torso, one hand going to his nipples and the other to his belly and cock, getting close in, squeezing myself into him the way I liked it. My teeth pressed into the side of his neck, as I entered his ass. He trembled under me in a mixture of anticipation, pain, and pleasure as my eight and a half inches plowed their way toward the center of him. My skittish little thoroughbred racehorse. This time he was very vocal, telling me that I was filling and stretching him to the limit in the most incredible fucking he'd ever had. Grunting and groaning, and sighing and moaning, and screaming for me to fuck his brains out.

He was incredibly tight, just the way I wanted it. When I had plowed him to the hilt, I started to pump him—slowly and deeply at first, and then with longer strokes. His ass walls came alive, their muscles undulating over my tightly encased cock as it stroked in and out. And it was so much better now than before, knowing that he wanted it this way too. After I'd cum in three separate gushes, I just sort of collapsed on top of him as he was draped over the toilet, but I heard no objection from him. He was loving the close embrace as much as I did.

After several minutes, we showered together, in a close embrace under the streaming water. He took my cock in both of his hands, and, incredibly, it was coming to life again. I did him there, for a third time, without restraints and without lube or condom, skin rubbing against undulating ass walls. He now understood my need for closeness and tightness and control, and he now just let me push him into the corner of the shower stall, the water raining down on us and running over us, as I put my hands under his hips, with him facing me, and lifted his body and lowered his pelvis onto my fat, long skewer. He wrapped his legs tightly around my hips and buttocks, holding me close into his tight ass canal, his arms wrapped tightly around my neck, our heaving chests nipple to nipple and belly to belly, and he held still as I pumped him until he had shot cum up my belly between my pecs and I had cum once more, bareback, eight and a half inches up his ass.

Nathan and Jack's Blind Date

It was 2:00 p.m. Jack was hungry and, if the wind picked up any more, he'd be cold as well. Both things made him grumpy.

"Sorry I'm late." The man's cry was almost carried away by the wind.

Jack turned and saw the guy hurrying along the jetty toward him, jacket flapping about him and carrying a plastic bag in one hand and the other trying to hold on to some kind of hat. Jack realised it was a nautical captain's hat. A dork. That was his impression of the guy now that he saw him in the flesh, and that was added to his growing annoyance with having agreed to this date. It was the guy's serious profile, his shyness online, and the promise of a cruise around Sydney harbour on an otherwise empty Sunday that had made him accept. A scenic cruise and, well, whatever came next. Maybe a blow job to show he was appreciative. Maybe more. Now he was tossing up just walking away before the date even started.

"I brought hot food for lunch, as was arranged," the guy added, now almost next to Jack. "Sorry I'm late. Nathan, that's me, sorry again, work. I picked up the food on the way." He lifted up the carry bag, obviously full of something hot. Then he ushered Jack onto the deck of the small cruiser and stepped on after him. Nice boat Jack thought, not big, not a luxury party boat, but ideal for a couple of people to cruise the harbour in summer and fish and swim from and maybe overnight on.

"So, Jack, I hear you have a couple of hours to see how she goes on the harbour. She is a nice steady boat. Hardly used. And the price is negotiable. We have to have lunch, though, so food first, or would you rather we headed into the harbour?" Nathan asked, as they entered the main deck and wheelhouse with a table and benches as well as the controls in it.

Jack was a bit confused. "You are selling this boat?" Jack asked, "and you think I am interested in buying it?"

Nathan looked at him with a lost expression on his face. "Yes, um, that was what I was told. Ah . . ."

"OK, yes. I'd like to see the boat in action. But food first, I think." Jack was happy to go along with whatever was going on. He was also turning over in his mind the online exchanges that had led up to this date. Lots of I am an ordinary guy, I am fit and healthy and like the home life, and I am looking for something permanent. Somehow it had never come up that he was trying to sell him a boat. Maybe the guy had confused his dates. Jack smiled, thinking about it, and was curious to let things run for a bit, especially if he could escape after eating.

"A bit of heat, I think," Nathan said, glancing furtively at Jack while switching on a small heater. He sloughed off his coat, and before Jack could see what he looked like without it Nathan had slipped down the steps into the small galley. Past that Jack looked through to the cabin with a huge bunk, not the usual two V'd bunks he expected.

"I hope you like Thai."

Actually Jack was not keen on Thai, having recently had a bad experience with a Thai green curry that had lasted a couple of days. Warm air started to flow into the wheelhouse, which was the first plus since he had arrived at the yacht basin.

"Oh sorry. It's not Thai. Looks like Sal got something else. Um, fish and chips and calamari rings and scallops. Sorry. No idea what she was thinking."

Jack was relieved he was being spared Thai and he liked fish and chips. It was not something he usually admitted to people he met as it was rather uncool, he knew. It was a bit like saying you liked McDonalds. But on his own if he wanted takeaway, that was usually his first choice. And he thought it was on his Internet profile. Favourite food: fish and chips.

"That's fine," he called down. "Who is Sal?" he added.

The situation was already weird and he always preferred to know right off if a date had a female in his life, if he leant only one way or both. If the guy could get his dates muddled maybe he wasn't even sure he liked men.

"Good, good." Nathan appeared at the stairs, bounded up them like an eager puppy, and laid a plate piled with steaming small pieces of battered fish and chips on the table. He looked at Jack nervously. "Fish and chips, I like them too, but . . . not cool," he said before he disappeared down the steps again and reappeared with another steaming plate. "Calamari and scallops."

Jack finally got a proper look at Nathan and he looked like his profile pics. So, at least he was NorthernCruiser. He had wondered for a moment if he was the one who had somehow gone to the wrong date.

"And Sal?" Jack asked pointedly.

"Sal? Oh, my niece. She was the one who arranged for you to look at the boat today. Said a cruise around the harbour would give you a good idea of what sort of boat she is. And lunch. Sal said you had told her you would not have time to eat if you had to be here at two."

Jack was starting to put the pieces together. "Sal said I was interested in buying your boat? And told you to bring lunch?"

"Um, yes. Um . . ." Nathan looked confused again. "Yes. You are interested in buying a boat, aren't you? I mean Sal said . . ."

Jack could see that Nathan was trying hard to be politely business like, but he kept taking sideways looks at him. Those kind of interested looks, he was sure. The only question was would he straighten things out for Nathan before or after they ate? He looked at the food and picked up a bit of fish.

"So, how long have you had the boat? and why are you selling?" he asked.

"Three and a half years. I always wanted a boat, but once I had one I never seemed to have the time to go out on her. Work. I work for myself. And you, what are your plans for the boat?"

Jack thought a moment. "I would like an excuse to get out for the day. Like you, I am busy and I live alone, so I spend too much time on business. And a boat seems like a good idea." Now he had said it he realised it was true. He did spend too much time working, and as he'd got older he went out less and met fewer men and so on. Not that he was likely to meet many new men if he cruised around the harbour in the summer with people he already knew.

"Ah," said Nathan, "I live alone too, not far from here. But it's too easy to get up and turn on the computer and start to work on the weekends instead of . . ."

Jack smiled. He could have said much the same himself, though his problem was living only a short walk from the business. He looked at Nathan sitting there looking serious and eating his food slowly and carefully.

"Nathan, do you have a profile on the Harbour Boys site? NorthernCruiser."

Nathan's mouth fell open and he went red as a beet.

"I also have a profile on Harbour Boys," said jack. "And I think Sal has set us up. I got contacted by you, and you arranged for us to meet here today for a date, like a get-to-know-each-other date. Arranged through Harbour Boys."

Nathan's mouth half closed and moved around, but no sound came out. Jack picked up a piece of fish. "Let's not let it get cold," he said.

"Sal?" Nathan said, then took up a chip and ate it thoughtfully, the red fading from his face and neck. "So, you are not here because you are interested in buying the boat? You didn't see the ad on eBay?"

The red had been refreshing to see, Jack thought. Nice to meet a man who could be genuinely embarrassed and one who looked average, but fit, not trying too hard to look younger or anything else. He was also going over what he remembered of Nathan's profile on line and was struck by a sudden worry. "Did Sal write up your profile for you?" he asked.

"No, no of course not," Nathan replied, looking shocked at the idea. "I mean she knows I am gay. But . . . well I hope she didn't . . ." He flushed again and dug around in his jacket until he produced a mobile phone. "I think I had better check," he said, stabbing at the screen.

"So, you have not seen my profile?" Jack asked.

"No, no," Nathan looked up frowning. Then he was busy scanning the screen. "Hmm, she has changed a few things. Hmm." He raised his eyebrows and shook his head slightly. "Hmm. You came after seeing my profile?"

"Yes."

"Should I see yours?" Nathan asked, frowning again.

"No, I don't think that is necessary. It's interesting to be unknown for a change." Jack felt a certain charge from discovering that Nathan knew nothing about him, while he knew a great deal about Nathan, even if edited by Sal. "And Sal picked me out, so . . ." he added with a laugh. "Let's get comfortable and pretend I really am here to buy the boat."

Nathan looked relieved to have something normal to focus on. "Oh, the boat. It's a good boat, all the latest safely gear. Four berths, but two are up here with the table folded down. I never get time to come out on her, though." He leant back on the bench seat. "I have never spent a night on her. In fact this is probably only the fifth time I have been out in her. But I come down every couple of months to make sure she is still here. Looked after." He paused.

Jack was enjoying the food and the cabin was warm now. Nathan was looking at him with a look of intensity that was obvious curiosity and definite interest. He knew he had been curious about Nathan from the start, even though it now seemed it was Sal he had been having exchanges with in setting up the date. Jack smiled to himself. Things were not so bad after all, but he needed to know more.

Jack looked directly at Nathan and leant towards him across the table, licking each of his fingers slowly, taking off the salty fat left by the fish he had eaten.

Nathan caught his breath and began to pant. "You are playing with me, Jack," Nathan said in a husky voice.

Jack smiled. "I think it's time to find out if we are suited." He leant over and laying a hand behind Nathan's head pulled his face to him and their lips met for a slow, salty kiss.

Jack wondered what it would be like to drag Nathan over the table and fuck him right then, but was not one to rush things.

Nathan surprised him by putting a hand behind Jack's neck and continuing the kiss, taking it deeper, their tongues dueling for occupation of the other's mouth, Jack winning. Without breaking the kiss, Jack moved around the small table to the opposite bench that Nathan sat on and sat beside him. One hand stayed on the back of Nathan's head, while the other snaked to his crotch and Jack found how interested Nathan was.

When his hand held Nathan's basket through his pants, Jack broke the kiss and looked into Nathan's eyes. "Christ," he gasped. "What was on your profile before Sal got at it?"

"Um, yes," Nathan replied his eyes slitted. "Eight and a half inches, and thick. No idea why she took that out and put average instead."

Jack was unzipping Nathan's pants and pulling the still-growing cock free to stroke. Nathan reached for Jack's crotch and unzipped him and reached inside and groaned. "Oh man." Then he laughed, his hand fisting Jack's cock as it grew to a thick eight and a half inches for him.

"I think your Sal got things wrong putting two tops together."

Nathan continued stroking Jack's cock and pulled his head in for another kiss, his breathing heavy and his body moving against Jack's. "Maybe not so wrong." Nathan murmured and a moan escaped him before he returned to the kiss, letting Jack's tongue take possession of his mouth.

Jack came up for air and began unbuttoning Nathan's shirt, but he stopped, pulled away, and stood. He grabbed Nathan's hands and pulled him out of the bench seat, faced him toward the stairs down to the cabin, pressing up behind him. Nathan groaned but managed to go down the stairs and throw himself back on the big bunk. Jack looked down at him lying there, arms flung out, Nathan's huge cock rising from his pants, fat and throbbing. Then he stepped down and pulled Nathan's pants and briefs off his legs and knelt over him.

As Jack undid Nathan's shirt and began to kiss down his body, licking through the tangle of hair around his nipples and running down his belly to his bush, Nathan was stripping off Jack's clothes roughly, running his fingers through Jack's hair and then around his shoulders and down his back, pulling him in close and bending his legs to encase Jack between them.

Jack's mouth reached Nathan's cock and he did his best to make love to it. A beautiful, thick, long cock different to his own, yet similar. He had rarely seen, and never made love to, one like it before. Men came to him to be fucked by him, men who had rarely been close in size. Part of him doubted Nathan could really take him. But he pushed the thought away, knowing he wanted to take him.

Nathan was moaning and rock hard and throbbing and lifting his legs to give Jack access to his hole. Jack blew on it and licked it, seeing it loosen. He fingered it—one, two, then three fingers. Nathan's moans got louder, and he was lifting himself up on his elbows to look down at Jack between his thighs. "I want it, I want to see it," he growled. He reached down and grasped Jack's hair and pulled his head up till they kissed. "I want to taste you," he said, his eyes fixed on Jack's.

Jack moved up so Nathan could take his cock in his mouth and do his best to taste it all before falling back. "Take me, now," Nathan gasped.

Jack returned to Nathan's hole and Nathan spread and raised his legs, planting his feet on the lower roof at the sides of the cabin. But he also lifted himself up on his elbows again wanting to see that huge dick making its way into him, see it disappear as he had seen his own disappear in other men. Wanting to know what it was like to be taken by something so big. Jack had dug lube and a condom out of the pocket of his pants and now crowned himself and spread the lube on his cock and began to finger it into Nathan's hole.

The two men's eyes locked as Jack placed the head of his cock at the entrance to Nathan's channel and began to work it in. Nathan's hole resisted and Jack leant forward and bit his nipples sharply, making the man under him writhe and spout his cream. And his hole relaxed and began to let him in.

Nathan looked down his body again, and seeing that part of Jack's cock was now inside him, he threw his head back and panted and tried to relax, wanting it all inside. Knowing it would be painful this first time, but wanting it.

Jack lost control as soon as he bottomed, fucking in long, deep strokes, Nathan cried out and bucked under him, making the ride wilder. Nathan shot his second load at about the same time Jack lost his first inside him.

* * * *

"So, where do you want to be in five years?" Jack asked, lying on his side with Nathan cuddled into his body.

"Right here," Nathan replied with a sigh. "And you?"

"Oh, I want to be president of my own company and happily married."

Nathan tensed.

"Actually, I *am* president of my own company, and I hope in five years they will have legalised gay marriage in Australia," Jack added, kissing the back of Nathan's neck.

"What sort of company?" Nathan asked.

"Actually, the one you have just completed a big contract for," Jack replied. "That was what made me curious enough to go on a blind date with you, when I caught on to who you probably were. You did a fantastic job for us. I wanted to meet you then but was overseas so didn't get a chance. Then you, or I should say Sal, contacted me, and . . . you know the rest."

Nathan turned his head and looked at Jack. "You? Your company, you're . . ."

Whatever he was going to say was cut off by the feel of Jack rubbing a rehardened cock across his entrance.

Public Warrior Dating

"Fuckin' shit. Here, take this. Not a word about the other one," Tom said gruffly, as he shoved the paper bag containing a sealed bottle of vodka over into my lap. In the same motion he was pushing the opened pint bottle under his seat. In the flashing of the blue light bouncing off the dashboard of his Dodge Ram, I could clearly make out the "oh, shit" expression on his face.

I'd been worried he was driving too fast and swigging vodka too much, so it was somewhat of a relief to me that we were being pulled over. It was an "oh, shit," moment for me, though, because I didn't know now whether I was going to get what I'd built up the courage over the past few weeks to seek out. His raw and overbearing behavior was arousing—it was much of what I imagined I was after in going on this blind date.

We'd hooked up for a blind date on Craigslist, getting pretty explicit what we wanted before we agreed on a date. My affair, if you could call it that, with Professor Teller was OK, but I was itching to try something more adventuresome, rougher—I wanted to try a bigger cock, one with more vigor and stamina, if truth be known. Somebody more controlling and raw. Also muscles—and youth.

The professor was amorous enough and certainly long enough, but he was nearly three times my age and so delicate and sensitive about everything. He insisted on doing it on clean sheets and with nearly the same fastidious pattern to it each time. The same few positions. Just once, I'd like him to fuck me wildly on his kitchen table on top of the breakfast service. But I'd never even been there at breakfast, and I doubted he could survive to lunch if he tried it.

I wanted to try a construction worker type or someone like that, someone who worked hard with his body and thus was hard bodied—and maybe a bit crude. Something different. I wanted to be taken—ravished—not just fucked.

Tom posted that he was a construction worker and volunteer fireman, twenty-eight, and into bodybuilding, all of which spelled "bingo" to me. His language was direct and his misspellings and frequent use of "fuck" in his Internet postings showed a welcome and risk-taking contrast to the fastidiousness of Professor Teller. He very directly stated that he was eight inches, cut, and thick and was looking for a submissive.

Fireman. Maybe just the ticket. My eyes had gone up to the New York Firemen beefcake calendar I had on the wall behind my computer. Yeah, a fireman. Maybe just the ticket.

It all spelled out what I wanted to try as relief from the norm. Still, it had taken three weeks for me to agree to meet after we'd exchanged photos and he said he was interested—and would take care of the date. He was quite direct in how he expected the date to end up and that he'd book a motel room.

"If you won't bottom for me and don't want me to fuck the shit out of you, don't bother to come," he'd written.

We were on our way to the motel room when the cop pulled us over.

* * * *

But that's not how the evening started. Tom picked me up in front of the college library and took me to a sports bar for dinner while we watched a pro basketball game on the overhead TV. He was much into the game, and I pretended to be even though I don't follow basketball and didn't have a clue who was playing. It must have been a gay bar, because he pawed me while most of his attention was going to the TV screen and no one around us seemed to be disconcerted about that. By halftime he knew about all there was to know concerning my body and he'd made sure I knew he, indeed, was thick and hung. He'd crammed my hand below his waistband so I'd know none of that down there was padding.

"Nice, very nice," he'd said more than once when he was doing his survey, which made me want to purr. I shuddered when he said, "Small. Like them small. Bet you've got a tight hole," but that had aroused me as well.

Then there was an hour of pool, where I did know a thing or two about the game, but made sure that he came out the victor. I was prepared to let him be the victor in everything. He was self-assured and cocky and, at least on the physical level, had every reason to be so. A big-boned Nordic blond, built solid, and with a strut. He went out of his way to muscle in on me during the pool, and I yielded to everything. He liked showing me how I should hold the pool cue, which gave him the opportunity to cover me from behind and let me feel his bulge against my buttocks. I could tell that he was testing me and that was what he wanted. He was no genius in the mental realm, but if I had wanted a steady diet of genius, I'd have been completely satisfied with the professor.

He seemed to need to signal to the others in the pool area that "I'm taking this one home and fucking him," but I didn't mind that. It was exactly the adventure I was after. I wanted steam, demanding power and control, and a whopping big churning cock inside me—at least for a change—and there was every indication that the fireman hunk, Tom Fielder, was going to give that to me.

Normally I might have thought he was overcompensating with his bravado, but he'd made sure I had gotten the measure of him early in the date and when I got into his car, he reached over, took my hand, and laid it on his basket and said, "I wasn't lying about what I was packing. If you can't handle this, there's no reason to do this date."

As coolly as I could I asked him what, if anything, we were going to do that evening before he fucked me. What he told me did include a stop on the road by a cop.

* * * *

"Evening, sir. May I see your license and registration, please." The voice was deep and in control—polite but no nonsense. What I had seen as he walked up to Tom's side of the truck was tall, dark, and handsome. Also muscular, and he walked with confidence and a bit of wariness, keeping his hand on his gun holster, the holster unsnapped. He filled his police uniform arrestingly well. He had a flashlight that he beamed at Tom's face, as much for defense as identification, I thought. It was a long one but not as thick as most flashlights I'd seen except in at the bulb end. It illuminated his face for me too, though. Strong, chiseled features, five-o-clock shadow of black hair on his lower face, laugh lines around the hazel eyes, deep tan. A rugged, but strikingly handsome and confident face.

"Something wrong, officer?" Tom asked, his voice a bit tight, as he reached over my knees to open the glove compartment and take out the registration. I could see—and hoped the cop couldn't—that while getting at the registration Tom had to make sure that the pistol in the glove compartment was hidden behind the service booklets. I felt a tightening in my chest. But I also felt a bit of arousal. I had been looking for adventure, and I felt I was in a thriller movie.

Tom gave me a "I know you see it, but you don't see it, do you?" look and I gave him my best "you're the boss, whatever you want" submissive look in return.

"Well, you were driving at least fifteen miles over the speed limit back there," the officer said, as he turned the beam of the flashlight on Tom's license and registration cards.

"Uh, sorry. Occupational hazard, I guess," Tom answered. "No one else on the road, though, so I just slipped into it. I can keep it down from here. Not far to go."

"Occupational hazard?"

Tom pointed to the red light case on his dash. "Fireman. I get locked into a need to get there fast. You know how it is."

"Ah, a public warrior," the policeman said. "Guess that can slide, as long as you try to keep it down to your destination. You're not drinking, though, are you?" he asked, his light now shining on the unmistakable shape of the bagged pint bottle in my lap.

"No, sir," Tom answered. "On my way to a party, but the bottle is sealed. Show him the bottle, Chris."

I pulled the neck of the vodka bottle out of the bag for the officer to see. The beam of light went from that to my face.

"You say you don't have far to go?" the officer asked Tom.

"Just over on Taylor Creek Road; just a few blocks away." About the only place there was to go to a party on

Taylor Creek Road was the Wildwood Motel, a notorious rent-by-the-hour fleabag.

The light came back up onto my face. "How old are you, son?" the office asked.

"Nearly twenty, officer," I answered, trying to keep the nervous squeak out of my voice.

"You got a license I can see?"

"Sure," I said, digging it out and handing it to him across Tom's chest.

He looked at it in the beam of the flashlight. "Chris Collins. Address over by the college. You a student there?"

"Yes, sir," I answered.

"And you're good with this ride you're taking?" he asked.

"Yes, sir," I answered.

"Well, you drive more carefully now, Fireman Tom," the officer said, "And keep in mind that you're not the only one in the car or on the road when you're driving."

"Sure will keep that in mind," Tom answered through tight lips. I could tell that he didn't like the lecture at all.

We both watched the policeman saunter back to his car—probably with different thoughts in mind. Tom was muttering, "Arrogant son of a bitch," under his breath. I was thinking about how tight the man's butt was and how muscular his thighs looked in those tight trousers.

"Cocky bastard," I said under my breath but loud enough for Tom to hear. It wasn't anything I meant, but I thought it would assuage Tom's ego, and it seemed to. He relaxed the fists he was making on the steering wheel.

If anything, the police stop had made me more horny than ever for what the cop called a public warrior booty call. I reached over and palmed Tom's package as he revved up the car. I knew he'd felt emasculated in front of me by the cop's presence and control of the situation.

"I want you to fuck me good at the motel," I murmured, trying to move him back into a dominating swagger.

"I'll fuck your lights out," he growled as he let the engine rumble longer than necessary before putting it into gear and moving away from the revolving circle of blue light.

* * * *

Indeed, Tom, the hunky and primeval fireman, did fuck my lights out at the motel—roughly and demandingly just as I had wanted and nervously looked forward to. He wasn't all bravado; he delivered.

I knelt between his legs, both of us naked, his body hard-bodied muscular and smooth skinned other than the blond bush at the pubes, and gagged at being forced to try to deep throat eight thick inches of him while he held my head close into his groin. He knew I was having trouble with it and was gagging, but he just kept on holding my head and pushing himself down my throat. I kept telling myself that I'd wanted to try it this rough.

We'd already finished off the pint of vodka Tom had started—or, more correctly, Tom had finished it off; I'd had half a Dixie cup full of the booze, but I was trying to keep on the clear side of a buzz as I didn't want to miss any sensation of this long-anticipated fuck. We'd already had several beers at the sports bar—Tom more than me— before stopping at the liquor store when we left the bar for the motel.

He was slurring his words, but it certainly didn't cut into his ability to gain and maintain a mammoth erection, his sexual athletic ability, or his mastery of control. Just when I didn't think I could take any more of his cock pushing at the back of my throat, he leaned over, grasped my waist between his hands, and with a "Whoopsy do,"

91

raised, turned, and flipped me. He had me by nearly a hundred pounds and six or seven inches in height and wingspan, so he manipulated me with ease. That, as much as anything else, I found highly arousing, and I was as hard as a rock and panting. Tom was rock hard too, if not panting. He handled me like he totally debauched a small guy like me three times a week, and, for all I knew, he did. He certainly left no doubt that I had been royally fucked.

Before we had started he'd casually laid three Trojan Magnum condom packets out on the nightstand along with a can of lube—all in a line, natural as you please, and he'd grinned at me when I shuddered. I'd involuntarily moved a bit from him where we were sitting side by side on the bed, but he'd reached out, pulled me roughly to him, and held my back into his chest, with a hand cupping my chin and pulling my head back into the hollow of his shoulder. He undressed me with his other hand—he remained dressed—unbuttoning my sports shirt and pulling it off my back and unbuckling and unzipping my jeans and pushing them down to my knees. I was going commando, which he seemed to appreciate. He fisted my cock and I squirmed ineffectually in his embrace as he jerked me off. There was no question that I was going to arc my cum for him, and I did.

"That's you; the rest is all me," he growled.

Then he'd pushed me over on the bed, propped up on my elbows; stood between my spread knees; and stripped off his own clothes. He took up the bottle of vodka from the nightstand and took several swigs as I started sucking his cock and balls in that position. It was only after a bit that he pushed my face away, sat on the side of the bed, put me on my knees between his thighs, and started controlling the serious deep throating, which lasted until he'd grown just too thick and long to handle.

When he pulled me up and reversed and flipped me, I came down with my shoulders on his thighs and my legs waving in the air in the splits. I grabbed for his ankles as, pushing at my butt cheeks with his facial cheeks, he went for my asshole with his mouth. He slathered me up good there, getting lube and his fingers into the process, and muttering, when he'd moved to using his fingers, "Open for me. You'll want to be open. Relax. Yes. Give it to me. Open up. Want you tight, but don't want to split you."

It's a little hard to open up your channel when you're upside down and your legs are doing the splits. I'd never been in a position like this before. But he was strong and holding me in place. I at no time thought I was going to fall over. In fact, he pulled me up and swallowed my cock as he took a break from eating my ass out, which brought my head up into his lap and put me in a position to give his cock more suck too.

"Ummm, nice," I heard him say after a while. "That should be good for starters. I want it tight anyway."

He then flipped me again and set me down on his thighs as he reached over for a condom, rolled it on, and lubed it up. I could feel the huge cock at the small of my back as he prepared it. I began to hyperventilate as he grabbed my waist, lifted me, and set my passage opening down on his cock. I wasn't nearly open enough to take him yet, but he was ready to fuck me, so that's what happened.

I squirmed and panted and whimpered and almost sobbed, while he muttered for me to relax and open to him and relentlessly pressed me down on his cock.

"Hey, you said you've done this before. You weren't shitting me, were you?"

"Yes, I've done it. Just not this big," I managed to croak out for him. That seemed to be good enough for him. I certainly didn't get the feeling he was cutting me any slack after that.

I struggled to accommodate the shaft and then found myself stretching and taking him. When I felt my butt cheek pressing into the curls of his pubes, he embraced

93

me closely and gently rocked back and forth for a few brief moments. The longer we rocked the more open I was to him and the thicker he became, until I felt comfortable enough to turn my face to his for a deep kiss.

"Just relax now," he whispered. "Go limp and let your body fall forward between our legs. Grab my ankles or knuckle the floor. I don't care which. Leave it to me. Just give me your hole and stay open for me. I'm gonna' fuck you like you've never been fucked before."

And then he did just that, pulling me on and off his cock, at first slowly and deeply, but quickly increasing the speed and the vigor of the fuck—pulling me on and off the cock for a good fifteen minutes before he tensed, jerked, and filled the bulb of the condom.

He pulled me off the cock immediately and tossed me over onto the bed on my back. Then he stood, turned full frontal to me—with me gasping again at how muscular and hung he was—and smiled as he pulled the spent condom off his cock and dropped it in a wastebasket.

"That was a good one. You're a sweet sub," he said, as he reached for the bottle of vodka and took a deep swallow. "And a nice, small bod. I want to watch you jerk yourself off now."

So, I did that for him, lying on my back, legs spread and bent, my eyes watching his as I masturbated and he fondled and stroked his still-half-hard cock. When he was hard again, I watched him pull on the second condom and then he was on top of me on the bed, turning me over, slapping my legs up onto my knees, my thighs spread. He crouched over my back, mounted my ass, thrust inside me, and power fucked me for another fifteen minutes.

I rolled over onto my side in satisfied exhaustion as he came off the bed.

"I'll shower and then you can and I'll drive you back to your apartment," he said, adding, "Nice fuck. I'll want to nail you again."

I turned my eye to the nightstand and the third condom—not that I was that anxious for him to fuck me again; he'd pretty much worn me out, but very satisfactorily so. His eyes followed mine, and he laughed.

"No, I'm not finished with you tonight. Want to do you under the stars in the bed of my truck, though. I'll find somewhere on the way to your apartment. Give you a little romance. Won't that be nice?"

"Yeah, sure," I mumbled.

"And give you all eight thick inches again. Won't that be somethin'?"

In answer, I moaned and threw my arm over my face. He laughed, scooped his clothes off the floor, and headed for the bathroom.

* * * *

"Here, this looks like a good place to pull off for a little . . . oh, shit. Fuckin' shit!"

The blue light was pulsating off the dashboard again. And this time Tom was obviously drunk as a skunk and was driving erratically. I'd been wondering if he even could perform if he got me in the bed of his truck, and I had still been mulling whether I regretted it if he couldn't get it up again. I'd had the rough, athletic fuck by a hung hunk that had sent me into this blind date. Had I had enough to be satisfied now? He was getting a little ugly.

"It's a cop car—no, two of them," I said, looking around to the car following us—and the car following that one. "Aren't you going to—?"

"Shut the fuck up. Did I ask you your opinion?" he growled, and as he did so, a hand came off the steering wheel and he backhanded me across the mouth. I fell back against the passenger door, and my hand shot up to my mouth, feeling for damage. But, although, it stung, I didn't feel a cut or blood. Still, the unexpected violence of it raised

95

mixed sensations. I was shocked, yes, but I also was aroused. I felt myself harden up. If he'd been in a position to follow the hand strike by falling upon me, I knew my hands would go to his cock to pull him inside me. And that scared me.

For the briefest moment I thought he was going to stomp down on the accelerator and try to outrun them, but then he hit the steering wheel with the same fist he'd hit me with, muttered, "Fuckin' hell. Shit. Fuck, fuck, fuck," and pulled over to the side of the road.

Turning to me as one cop car stopped behind us and the other one pulled around in front of us, Tom said, "Keep your fuckin' mouth closed. We did nothin', you hear? That license you showed him is fake, isn't it? You're sixteen, ain't you?"

"No, I'm not. The age on the license is right," I stammered out.

"I said not to fuckin' say a word," he said. "There's some reason they stopped us. They been waitin' for us to leave the motel."

I wanted to scream that they stopped us because he was drunk on his tail and using both lanes of the road to drive on, but I dared not say anything else.

"You open your yap and I swear I'll beat you to a pulp."

I just nodded my head, scary visions going through my head of Tom slapping me around, both of us naked, and then fucking me—and me liking it. Had I opened some sort of Pandora's Box of my fetish preferences with this blind date?

By then, though, one of the cops was at the window and the other was standing in front of Tom's truck, his gun half out of his holster, his other hand holding some sort of communications device to his mouth. He already was calling the license plate number in. The cop at the window was the same dark hunk who had stopped us before.

"Need you to get out of the truck, nice and easy, Mr. Fielder," the cop said.

"What the shit? I ain't—"

"You've been driving erratically," the cop said. "And I can smell the alcohol from here. Your little party is over now. You get on out of the car now. Larry here will take you in to spend the night in a comfy cell and sober up. We'll treat you right as a public warrior; just let you walk in the morning. Nothing on paper. That is, if you don't give us any shit on this. It'll be good for you and for everyone else on the road tonight."

The cop wasn't paying any attention to me and I sank down a bit in the seat. I wasn't any sort of public servant hero. There'd be no reason not to write me up— although I couldn't think of anything I'd done that was illegal. Guilt by association, I guess.

Tom slid out of the car easily enough, allowed the cop to cuff him, and the two cops to walk him back to the cruiser parked in front. Tall, dark, and handsome came back and stood by the fender of the truck and watched the other cop car drive away. I watched through the windshield. I had no idea what would happen then. I'd had some to drink too. And I was sitting here in Tom's truck. The keys were in the ignition, but this wasn't my truck. We were in a thinly populated area right outside a park entrance. My apartment by the college was more miles away than I wanted to walk at night.

Suddenly this blind date didn't seem the best of ideas.

"You been drinking too?" The cop hunk had come back to the car window and turned the beam of his long, thin flashlight on me. He didn't growl at me; he sounded calm, soothing. He'd dipped his head to look through the rolled-down window on the driver's side of the truck. A beefy forearm was propped up on the window sill—tanned, with curly black hair swirling around on it.

97

I stared at his eyes, not responding, and then looked away in submission, my attention going to the hair on his arm, wondering where else he had silky matting like that. He repeated his question, still in a calm voice. "You been drinking too, son?"

I shook my head. "Not more than one shot. I didn't want . . . sorry, officer. Tom told me not to speak and this is all just so different—a shock—to me."

"First time you've been with a man?"

I hesitated, but he was a cop. "No, sir, it's not."

"First time you went to a motel with this fireman dude?"

"Yes." I wanted to scream that I wasn't a rent-boy; that I was just in it for a different experience fling. but at that moment I did feel like a male whore.

"So, again. You been drinking too?"

"Yes, some, but this has sobered me up. Not much, though. One shot of vodka in the motel and a couple of beers at a sports bar before that—but that was a few hours ago."

"Relax. You weren't driving under the influence. No foul, as a passenger, if you can still walk a straight line. You can do that, can't you?"

"Yes, sir. You want me to do that for you?" I was eager to please. I knew I was sober enough to do that.

"I'll take your word for it. That's not what you can do for me. My name's Trane—that's my first name. I can tell you that because I've just gone off duty. And your name is Chris Collins, living over by the college. A college student, right?"

"Yes, sir."

"I'm off duty. You can call me Trane."

"Yes . . . Trane." That was the second time he'd told me he was off duty, like it was supposed to mean something to me, or something.

"You go with this guy because he was a fireman . . . a public warrior."

"Yeah, I guess. Curiosity, I guess."

"You go to the motel with him because you knew him and let him do you before or just because he was a built fireman?"

"I went with him mostly because he was a fireman—and young and muscular, I guess. I didn't know him. It was a blind date. I just wanted . . ." Hell, I couldn't tell him what I had wanted.

"But let's be clear. You let him fuck you, didn't you?"

"Yes, sir . . . Trane." I shouldn't have been embarrassed. I was old enough and it wasn't against the law. But I couldn't look into his eyes. I turned my face forward and stared out the front windshield.

"Your usual guy . . . the guy who usually fucks you . . . isn't young and muscular?"

"No. No, he's not."

"He all you hoped he would be, this Tom Fielder fireman?"

"Pretty much, I guess. Other than the drinking."

"Muscular, young . . . hung? Virile and vigorous?"

I didn't answer. This was getting a bit weird.

"Cops are public warriors too, you know."

"Yes." I certainly was aware of that. This hunk of a cop had my cock standing at attention.

"Well, now, we've got a problem. I can't let you drive this vehicle. It isn't yours. And I've got two vehicles out here. I can't drive the both back to the station. I think the best thing is for me to drive this truck into the park, leave it locked and in the parking lot there, and bring the key back to my cruiser. Then I can drive you home and take the key back to the jail to turn over to Mr. Fielder in the morning when he's sober and we cut him loose. Does that sound like a plan to you?"

"Yes, sir."

"Trane. Call me Trane. I'm off duty now."

"Yes, Trane, it sounds like a good plan. I wondered how I'd get home."

"I'll get you home. You want to ride into the park with me?"

"Yeah, I guess."

"The Fielder guy had his turning signal on. He was going to go into the park, wasn't he? He was going to take you into the park and do you again, wasn't he?"

"Yes."

"Just like he took you to that motel."

"Yes."

"Again, do you want to ride into the park with me? I'm sure I can do you as well as he did. I'm off duty."

I turned to look at him. He was running his hand up and down the shaft of the flashlight, like he was stroking it.

* * * *

Trane fucked me in the bed of the truck on a thin pile of army blankets we found back there. He stripped us both down and knelt at my chest, his beefy legs encasing my chest; one arm was stretched out gripping a handle at the base of the roofline behind the cab and his other hand was buried in the hair on my head, manipulating my head as his thick, long, hard cock stretched my throat.

If I'd had dreams of getting it rough, they were being fulfilled once again.

We were both naked, except that he was still wearing his equipment belt. He asked me if I'd like him to do that, and I answered that, yes, I'd like that—seeking the sensation of being fucked by another hunky public warrior.

He sat on the tailgate of the truck and bent me, naked, over his lap, holding my torso down with a strong arm across my back. After spanking me with his hand,

100

telling me to relax for him and given in completely, and he was convinced I was letting loose of all my tension and wouldn't fight him, he strapped my ass and thighs with my folded belt while I whimpered and sobbed in low tones until my ass must have blushed up. I didn't ask him to stop, though, and he could clearly see that it made me hard. I could feel that he was hard too.

"He did have a big one, didn't he?" Trane asked. He had more than one finger in my ass. "Reamed you big, he did." And then I gasped, gave a little yelp, and started panting hard, as he worked the butt end of his flashlight in me and twisted it and pumped it slightly.

"Oh, god, oh shit. Please," I whimpered.

"You gonna give me anything I want?" he asked.

"Yes, sir . . . yes, Trane. Fuck me . . . please."

Then, having made me demonstrate my surrender to him, he took me hard and rough, missionary style, me on my back, he on his knees between my bent and spread legs.

"Open to me. Take it," he demanded, and I complied. "Ah, yes, he opened you well."

Upon the first nailing of my ass, he gripped my waist between his hands and raised my pelvis to him, as he thrust inside me, to the hilt. He held there, with a fist at the small of my back, pressing and releasing, pressing and releasing, until I got what he wanted me to do. He was holding still, his gigantic rod deep inside me. He wanted me to signal my submission to him. I began to leverage off my feet, fucking myself on the hard cock, in long, slow strokes. He groaned his pleasure, my total surrender to him.

Hungrily, I fucked myself on his hard cock as he took my mouth in his in a deep kiss. I ran my fingers through the silky black curls on his hard, muscular chest. My mouth went there, licking his chest hair into swirly patterns and tonguing out his nipples and sucking on them as I moved my passage on his cock, taking him deeper into me as he thickened and lengthened. He had dog tags on a

101

chain around his neck, and when he released his kiss, I sucked those in my mouth and moaned my want, as I moved my pelvis against his, taking him as deep inside me as I could. I wanted to remember—to savor—this forever.

"Is it as big as the fireman's?" he demanded to know.

"Bigger," I answered through clinched teeth. And it was bigger—both thicker and longer.

When he had established who wanted what, he took control, holding me close in his embrace, as I moaned and groaned and he grunted in fucking me hard and fast and deep . . . and seemingly forever. Half way through the fuck, he turned me onto my forearms and knees, mounted me high on my buttocks, and fucked me like a dog. I would have barked for him if he had demanded I do so to keep the cock inside me and churning.

Stretched out beside me in the bed of the truck afterward, his arms embracing me, both of us looking up at the stars, and my moans only then beginning to subside, he asked, "Dorm or apartment?"

"Studio apartment. Not much. One room, really, with kitchenette and bathroom."

"Roommate?"

"No."

"Double bed?"

"More like three-quarters."

"Big enough. I'll be on top."

"Yes."

"You think you can stay with it all night?"

"I can certainly try."

Best damn blind date ever. Two public warriors in one blind date.

Japaneseartlover

Taylor was waiting. It was a date he had made on the Internet and they were hit and miss. Often the guy was chatting to more than just him and found someone who said right out "Come over to my place and fuck." Taylor was cautious. He had been caught out once doing that. A guy in biker gear had turned up rolling drunk and nasty with it. His profile had said he was a social drinker and an architect and the picture had been of someone else, he was sure, because though they both had dark hair and blue eyes, the one in his house was as tall as Taylor and a good fifty pounds heavier.

The biker stormed in and slapped him around and punched him, maybe thinking it was fun, but it certainly wasn't for Taylor, who could look after himself but was no match for a drunk who weighed a good fifty pounds more, felt no pain, and was used to using his fists.

Taylor had had trouble getting rid of the man and had spent a restless couple of nights worrying he might come back. It had put him off Internet hookups for several years, but his life had got so quiet he was dipping his foot back into it.

If the guy didn't show by nine, Taylor was going to head off to an art show opening. He hadn't been to one for a while, but the images of modern Japanese block prints in the poster advertising this one had really appealed to him. It had been put up on the gym notice board.

When nine o'clock came and the man had not shown up, Taylor felt relieved more than disappointed and left the café in a hurry.

* * * *

Clark was feeling extremely nervous and a bit guilty as he fussed around the exhibition space, checking that everything was hung straight and the labels on all the prints were the right ones. For some years now he had been doing his own version of the Japanese woodblock print and, as with those made in Japan, there was a story behind each block print that was hinted at in the picture's title and expanded on in the label. It was his first real exhibition and he had been increasingly nervous the closer it came to the big day.

"It looks very good," Javier said, smiling at Clark and also nodding at the people who were arriving in a steady stream for the opening. "Good to have something different. It seems to have caught everyone's imagination."

"Thank you," was all Clark could think to say. He was not sure how much he should work the crowd. He was no salesman and it was not something he liked to do. He often had to schmooze the clients in his work as an architect. Sometimes he enjoyed it and it was interesting, but at other times it was hard work and almost unpleasant. It depended on the clients. And he had to admit he had found several good lovers among them. He liked successful men who were in good physical shape and demanding.

Javier had moved on and was doing the schmoozing for him, Clark decided, watching him. Javier was good at it. He could smile and make almost anyone feel they were the centre of his attention. He also knew who was likely to buy a print. It was his gallery, and he was successful in a business that was hard to make a living at. Clark had had a brief fling with him when he had been designing the additions to the building. Both had turned out fine.

Clark surveyed the room, and a hand was raised up to beckon him over. He headed towards the group, which included several familiar faces. Once he was caught up in the social whirl, he relaxed, only discussing the prints when asked to.

He was returning to the bar for a second glass of wine when he saw a face that was familiar but that he could not place. Why he could not place him Clark had no idea, as seeing him made Clark's cock jump. The man had been looking closely at one of the prints, one Clark knew was fairly obviously representing a gay theme, before he turned around to survey the room, obviously looking for something. On impulse Clark went over to him. "Can I help you?" he asked.

"Ah, yes, I hope so," the man replied, in a deep voice like liquid chocolate. "Can you point out the artist or the gallery owner to me?"

"I am the artist," Clark replied.

The man focused on him and his eyes seemed to light up. "Wonderful. Nice to meet you . . ." He glanced back at the print, thick black strokes of ink representing bare tree trunks and the outlines of log houses with the white spaces being snow, ". . . Clark." Then the man smiled. It melted Clark. "My name is Taylor. You have caught the mood of the scenes perfectly. I am familiar with woodblock prints and usually dislike Western imitators, but in your case it works. You are not imitating the subjects but moving on to new ones, making use of the technique and style."

"I try," was all Clark could manage to say. He was standing with a man he was having trouble stopping himself from ripping the pants off. A man who also understood something of Japanese woodblock prints. He forced

105

himself to say something. "The mid-twentieth-century works appeal to me most," Clark added.

"Ah, the schools of Saito and Yoshida. I can see the inspiration. I personally collect earlier works, Hoshi and Maki, and some others."

Clark was caught between lust, curiosity, and a touch of envy. The prints the man had may be lithograph knockoffs. There were many good ones of the artists he had mentioned, but they might not all be and originals were rarely seen outside Japan. The man spoke quietly and turned again to Clark's print.

Clark was also racking his brain as to why the face was familiar. "You look familiar," he blurted out. "Have we met before?"

The man looked at him closely and seemed uncertain. "I am afraid I have a terrible memory for faces, but perhaps we have. I live in Richmond, but I often go to events here in Charlottesville. I saw the poster for this exhibition in the football team gym at the university."

"The team gym?" Clark was starting to form a thought and it was mind blowing. "Um you are not FootyTaylor from Gay Dates are you?" He asked. Unable to stop himself.

Taylor's eyes opened wide. "Why, yes. I waited for you till nine," he replied, frowning.

Clark was confused. "Waited for me?"

"Yes, you, Japaneseartistlover, at Gilligan's. Tonight."

Clark's head spun. "No, no, I am not Japaneseartistlover I am Japaneseartlover."

Taylor pulled out his mobile phone and rapidly tapped away. His face clearly turned a shade of pink and he looked up. "Apologies, Clark, you are right. I was waiting for the wrong man. Definitely the wrong man." He paused for a moment. "Would you like to go for a drink after this, and maybe see my print collection?" Taylor said seriously his hand moving to Clark's shoulder and then slipping down to his waist as his breathing deepened.

"You know that 'Come up to my place to see my prints' is a sexual come-on cliché," Clark said.

"Yes, but that's exactly how I meant it to be understood," Taylor answered, giving Clark a hard look.

Clark looked up at the chocolate-coloured giant and thought of the discussion they had had online the night before, how he had told Taylor he liked it long and thick and hard and forceful, and how Taylor had said that was just how he liked to do it.

"Definitely," Clark replied.

Three on a Date

I gingerly pulled Fraser's arm from across my chest and slowly moved my hips forward to pull my channel off his now-flaccid cock. There was nothing wrong with the length of him—that was his most notable feature for someone looking for sex from another man. He could remain deep inside me flaccid after a side-splitting fuck like we had just had. He was the only man I'd had who could reach deep inside me in a side split.

There wasn't much wrong with his looks and body, either, when his age and work life were taken into account. He was some twenty years older than I was and, being a department head at the Smithsonian Institution who lived for his work, he was soft except where it mattered most in sex. He wasn't fat; he, in fact, could go all day without food in the excitement of a new find or a developing exhibit for the American History Museum on the national mall, which, over the years, had led to him appearing gaunt.

He was tall, dressed elegantly, had once been quite handsome, and was both glib and witty. He had taken me under his wing when I'd first come to the Freer Gallery, across the mall from his museum but also in the Smithsonian system, right after completing a doctorate in art history and museum curating at Case Western Reserve in Cleveland, Ohio. We met at an orientation meeting for new Smithsonian employees. I was straight out of the Midwest. I wasn't naïve in terms of sex. I was actively gay but without hookups yet in D.C.

Fraser had given several orientation lectures for new Smithsonian employees in which he'd been witty and erudite and oh so welcoming. From the first lecture, he seemed to be looking at me as he spoke. We were introduced to each other and spoke sporadically and shallowly in the revolve of a cocktail party at the American History Museum Stars and Stripes café after museum hours. In one of our brief conversation groups, the question arose of whether any of us had tried out a new restaurant in Georgetown. Everyone in the group had, except me. Fraser said I must go—and that I must go that night after the cocktail party. And he would take me there. He said he wanted to know more about the program at Case Western Reserve anyway.

He was sparkling at the restaurant. We had another cocktail while waiting for our food and wine with dinner and port afterward. The conversation was easy and he an expert interviewer. I have no idea when I told him I was gay, but I did. Or when I told him I was unattached and at loose ends so far in D.C. Or when he first put his hand on my thigh under the table. Or when I told him that, yes, I found him attractive.

But I let him drive me home to my small apartment near Dupont Circle, come up to my bedroom, and wow me with how long it took him to uncoil his cock from his trousers and with how far he could put it up my channel. I'd never gone with an older man before, but in the dark, there was just him holding me close from behind, and that long cock of his. He took me quickly and efficiently with little foreplay or postcoidal cuddling. And then he got dressed and went home to his wife.

The next day he took me to lunch, again to a high-end restaurant in Georgetown. He apologized for the previous evening, saying we'd both had too much to drink and that he'd found me overpoweringly attractive. He said his wife, who was a Smithsonian archeologist, was frequently in the field and that they had a marriage of convenience—one that they were both happy in. But, he admitted, he had needs and sometimes acted on them—especially when she was gone. She, in fact, had left that morning for a dig in Egypt.

I sympathized with him, and after lunch, before we returned to work, he fucked me deep with that thin but long cock of his in the missionary position on my bed in my conveniently nearby apartment. He took me quickly and efficiently once again. The previous night had been in the doggy position leaning over my bed. Today was missionary. He had one other position—the side split—and he religiously worked his way through that pattern—doggy, missionary, side split—on Tuesday and Thursday noontime breaks in my apartment. Little foreplay, quick and efficient taking, and not much cuddling afterward—except, when his wife was out of town, he'd sleep in my bed on Sunday nights—one fuck following the pattern and then spooned sleeping in the bed—and give me a lift to the Smithsonian complex on Monday morning.

He had a parking space in a museum garage. I didn't. I took the subway. The Monday morning ride seemed worth the night before. The best part was sleeping with a long cock up inside me.

This was a Sunday night. He'd taken me to dinner—he was quite generous with that perk—come home with me, fucked me once on my bed—in a side split—and gone to sleep with my back burrowed in close to his spare frame, his cock going flaccid inside me.

As long as he was plowing me with that long cock, the coupling was fine. It was so scheduled and vanilla, though, that I was getting restless. I'd been in Washington, D.C., for five months and no one else had fucked me—no one younger than forty or muscular or spontaneous in his approach and carry through, or playful or even cruel.

I had fantasies of rough and cruel.

I had grown restless. I had done research. Research was what I was trained to do. I'd found a specialized subscription gay male dating site on the Internet. And I had paid for a subscription on Saturday, yesterday.

After extricating myself from Fraser, I padded out to the small room that had been rented to me as a second bedroom but that was little bigger than a closet. I used it as a home office. I turned on the computer and opened the home page of the specialized dating service I'd found. It was specialized because it set up dates of single men with male couples. Threesome dating. The service made no bones about the purpose of the date being sex, and its profile descriptions emphasized that.

I'd shot my load in an introductory perusal of the site Saturday night just in reading the profiles.

I'd never gone with two men before in a threesome. I hadn't done much of anything kinky before. There were a hell of a lot of sexual arrangements I hadn't tried before. And as time passed with Fraser, being denied anything that wasn't scheduled, vanilla, and over before I had had time to become deeply aroused, I began to feel more and more left out of the excitement of life. Fraser didn't seem to care if I had an ejaculation or not, as long as he did. So, increasingly, it wasn't happening for me every time.

The Web site made no bones about the goal being just dinner and a good-night kiss. The questioning for the profile was detailed and intrusive, although it was formatted mostly in a series of images of this and that, asking me to click on a scale of how much I was interested in this and that. The questions delved deep into fantasies and were constructed so that I was pulling much more out of my concept of desires than I'd even dared give thought to before.

The primary fantasy it brought out of me was being with two men at once. That was enough of a surface desire that I had sought out the dating service in the first place. I didn't know that would attract me when I started to look for something different than I was getting, but I knew it was something that attracted me as soon as I uncovered the Web site.

The questionnaire also was detailed in personal attributes, including both clothed and unclothed photos. I didn't have any trouble responding to that—either technically because I had shared nude photos with men when I was in Cleveland or in the need to hide anything. I had every reason to be proud of my physique, appearance, and equipment. Whereas most of the Smithsonian curators either took long, fattening lunches or ate at their desks while they worked, on Monday, Wednesday, and Friday I grabbed a quick salad at the museum café and then went to my nearby club and swam laps. On Saturday I worked out. I had kept myself in shape—great shape—while most who worked in my field sank into a mound of work-obsessed, unexercised Jell-O. And everyone told me that I reminded them of that "young movie heartthrob whatshisname," so I felt confident on the looks side of things.

The deal was that singles and couples signaled their interest to the Web site on the basis of the profiles made up from the questionnaires. If matches were found, dates were set up through the Web site, and the couple paid for the hookup. As a single I wouldn't pay for anything involving a match with a couple.

There weren't that many couples profiled on the Web site that hit all of my buttons. Many of them were older-younger pairs. There were a few, though, that had my cock bobbing, and that evening, while Fraser snored lightly in my bedroom, I pushed the "interested" button on four couples.

I closed down the computer and went back to bed. Fraser had turned over on his back. His flaccid cock curled along his thigh almost down to one of his knees. His legs were spread enough that I could sink between them. I had the strongest urge to do so and to give him a sensuous blow job he'd long remember.

But Fraser had made clear the first time that we fucked that he wasn't interested in such intimacy.

* * * *

The couple I was paired with were named Nash and Grant. Nash's profile was what attracted me first. Working as a horse breeder at a stables in the northern Virginia hunt country near Middleburg jumped right out at me. Beyond that I'd read biographies of the Kennedys. They'd kept a home in Middleburg so that Jackie could ride. I'd remembered that. I'd asked Fraser to drive me out there someday to see what the area was like, but he hadn't done so yet.

Of course both men were hunks, or I wouldn't have clicked on them. Nash claimed to be twenty-eight, two years older than I was. Grant listed at thirty-one. Nash was the muscle man. Blond; smooth-shaved all over, with a close-trimmed blond bush; cut (talking both body and cock here); rugged, chiseled features; just a couple of inches taller than I was; solidly built; an open, sunny smile. Big hands. Big dick. Not abnormally long, but really thick—what some term a Coke can cock. He wasn't erect in the photo, leading to the speculation on how he'd lengthen when aroused. Hefty balls, nestled close in under the cock.

His photos gave off the aura of aggressive stance, power, and straightforward honesty. I could see him working in the horse ring, shirtless, his muscular torso covered in a sheen of clean, musky-scented sweat.

Grant was quite a contrast to Nash. He was listed as an accountant and tennis club pro in Reston, an up-scale enclave township southwest of Washington, in Virginia, which had originally been built as a high-end, self-contained city set down in the countryside. Since then, Reston had been swallowed up by suburban sprawl, but it fought hard to maintain its separate identity.

Where Nash was blond and built powerful and close to the ground, Grant was dark, tall, and slim. He did have good muscular definition, but where Nash was sunny openness, Grant was sulky and sensuous, with a secretive aura. His hair was jet black and curly—and it covered much of his body—in arousing ways for anyone who liked hirsute men. And I did. If I had to characterize him in one word, it would be foxy. And I'd do so tapping into various aspects of that word. He looked to be highly intelligent—and the degrees he listed supported that—but he gave off the aspect of having secrets and being much smarter than anyone else in the room—both thinking he was and actually being right about that. I could see him as a schemer and cheat. Sexually, that didn't mean anything negative to me.

His hair appeared to be designed for modeling. Nash was clean shaven; Grant maintained what seemed to be a perpetual five-o'clock shadow. His chest hair swirled in a perfect pattern around nipples that protruded out noticeably, and the hair descended to his sculpted jet-black pubes in a thin line down his sternum and flat belly. His thighs and calves were heavily matted, as were his forearms, the knuckles on his hands, and the joints on his toes.

He cultivated the foxy and sensual look, facing the camera with a sneery smile, seeming to have pointed ears, and unabashedly exhibitionist, leaning back on some sort of credenza, his pelvis jutting out and sporting a full, upturned erection, the cock long, the ball sac hanging low between spread legs. A gay sex site shot; a would-be porn star.

Nash was listed as a top; Grant as versatile. I, of course, had listed as a bottom. That had been what was at the base of the matchup. There were other obvious matchups. My profile had said I was seeking adventure, variety, and testing—none of which I had explicitly stated. That must have been extracted from my choices of voting the scale on images the questionnaire presented. Their profiles indicated they were looking for—me. Most notably, I saw, because all three of us were listed as being willing to fuck on the first date and all three showed interest in double penetration. I certainly hadn't directly said I was. I'd have to think about that over the course of the date. Yes, of course I had fantasized about it—apparently in the questionnaire phase.

And all three had expressed an interest in big cocks, sports events, movie house sex, and barebacking. How the questionnaire had arrived at these for me mystified me. Disturbingly, I had apparently gone wild in filling the questionnaire out, no doubt from frustration with Fraser, showing interest in being controlled, bondage, and even flogging—acts I don't remember ever even thinking of before—but I must have if the questionnaire had pulled the desires out of me. And black bulls, exhibitionism, and gang bangs.

There seemed to be no end to the fetishes I'd allowed the computer to think I was interested in. And I suppose I'd always been curious and the frustration with Fraser had brought out the wanton in me. I couldn't deny that it gave me a hard on to read the list—and to contemplate the possibility that any of that would happen on a day of dating. There certainly would be no time to do it all. And, just as the questionnaires had brought out exaggeration from me, I'm sure it brought it out of these other two also. I had been permitted to review the list. My hand did hover over the edit button. But I was just so frustrated with the vanilla of Frasier and the lack of other opportunities beyond this dating service. I let the profile stand.

They came for me—by car—at a restaurant on M Street in Georgetown, just over Key Bridge from Roslyn, on the Virginia shore of the Potomac. Nash was driving a new red Mustang. Grant was in the backseat. They were controlling the date. For a day they were going to be controlling me. I couldn't have driven anyway. I didn't have a car in Washington.

Grant ushered me into the backseat with him, and Nash drove up Wisconsin Avenue, turned left onto P Street, pulled over to the curb, and let the car idle, as Grant turned and put an arm around my shoulders, pulling me close in beside him, and laid a hand on my package.

It was clear now and throughout the day that Grant was the leader and Nash the follower—and I the boy toy.

"So far so good," he said, "you're the same honey in the photos. But before we go any further, we need to establish what you'll do. If you don't stand behind the profile we bid on, we should know that now. You can get back out of the car here. We can get our money back for a date that doesn't get off the ground."

He was squeezing my package, his fingers ferreting out the balls, separating them, and giving them individual attention. I must have given him a pained, shocked look. I'd had no idea it would start this soon.

"You claimed interest in a whole lot of kinky stuff on your profile. You going to stand behind that? This isn't your normal date. Nash and I have paid a pretty penny for this. We will do a lot of what you showed interest in. We'll use you all day. We'll abuse you part of the day. If you don't want to deliver on your profile, it's good-bye here."

I was scared but I was exhilarated too. This was the jolt I had been seeking when I paid my $200 to register at the dating service. I didn't consciously know I wanted to experience these things listed in my profile. But I did. Even if it was the only one time.

"I'll stay in the car."

"Have you done all that shit listed in your profile?"

"Just some of it," I answered. "The questionnaire pulling those out were about desires—what I want to try."

"You'll do it all?"

"I'll stay in the car."

"Strip your jeans and briefs off," Grant commanded. "Before Nash starts to drive, strip down."

"Excuse me?"

"Gotta know if you're shitting us or if you're serious. Strip your jeans and briefs off. We're starting out at a horse show outside Middleburg. The date starts now. I'm going to do you back here while Nash drives us out there. Don't want that, get out of the car."

"I'm not wearing briefs," I answered as I started undoing my belt buckle. "You want my belt out of the loops or is it OK if I leave it in the trousers?"

"What?"

"Are you going to want to strap my ass with the belt or not?"

That set him back. He gave me a surprised look. "Not that; not yet," he said.

In the front seat, Nash laughed and pulled the car away from the curb, heading back down Wisconsin to M Street and then over Key Bridge into Virginia.

Grant was kissing me hard on the lips and jacking my cock with a fist before we hit the Virginia shore.

* * * *

After the forty-five-minute drive into the Virginia countryside during which Grant jacked me, I gave him a blow job, and I rode his cock, facing him, my knees pressed

117

into the fold where seat back met seat cushion on either side of his hips. All of this was hard to accomplish in the small backseat of a Mustang, but we managed. It helped that I had been a gymnast in college. Several hours of the remaining day, with a single exception, were downright staid, though—just what anyone would expect on a first date.

Except that my date was with two randy men, not one or with a woman.

"You had expressed an interest in sporting events, and Nash breeds and trains horses, so we thought you'd enjoy seeing a horse show and auction." Grant had seen the little smile I'd given when he'd said that as we got out of the backseat of the Mustang. Nash had popped out of the front seat and was striding toward a big horse barn with a riding ring behind it. Cars were parked haphazardly in the field Nash had parked in and people already were lining the rails of the riding ring. Beyond them I could see horses in the ring and handlers guiding them around.

"I see you reacted to Nash, horses, and breeding. Is that what attracted you to our profile on the dating service Web site? You clicked on interest in us first. We would have clicked on you—your photo and all of those kinks you were interested in—if you hadn't shown interest in us first. Your attention was arrested by riding and breeding and how Nash was hung?"

"I was attracted by how both of you are hung," I said. I surprised myself when I said that. I was determined to "get into" this date, even though it already was well outside my experience zone.

He laughed, drew me to him, and gave me a sloppy kiss on the lips. I looked quickly around to see if we'd been observed, but all of the attention seemed to be concentrated on what was going on in the riding ring.

"Never fear as far as Nash is concerned," he said. "Before the night is done, he will ride you and breed you.

118

We won you in an auction, and we're going to wear you out."

A shudder went up my spine—but one of anticipation and exhilaration.

By the time we got to the riding ring, Nash was already inside, leading a magnificent brute of a pure-white stallion around the ring. As they walked, the stallion must have seen a mare he wanted, because suddenly a thick pink tube of a cock started expanding between his hindquarters to become the definition of "horse-hung" cock. There were murmurs and snickers in the crowd, as Nash fought—and won—a struggle by the horse to get away from him and pursue its interests.

Two men, an older one and a much younger, were at the rail beside Grant and me. They were standing close, the older—obviously wealthy one—had a hand lightly pressed to the younger one's back. They were close enough to me that I could hear them converse.

"A magnificent beast," the younger one said, gesturing to where Nash was leading the stallion. "I'd love to ride that one."

"The stallion or the man?" the older one asked.

"They are both stallions, James," the younger one said, with a light laugh. "I was speaking of the horse. I've already been ridden by the man. A magnificent beast as well. Thickest cock I've ever taken. And he could ride all night."

The older man gave the younger one a sour look, turned away from him, and took a step away.

"Give over, James," the younger man said. "It was just a joke. Come back."

"Just a joke that Chuck Hastings has fucked you?"

"No, that part isn't a joke," the young man said. "Not a joke at all. Couldn't walk straight for two days."

The older man snorted and continued walking away.

So, his name wasn't really Nash, I thought. I guess I should have assumed that. I wasn't Ty either. I was Travis.

I turned back to watching Nash, if that's what he wanted to be called, in the ring. It was true that he was a magnificent beast. And to think that sometime in the next few hours he'd be fucking me. It caused me to go half hard and to tremble at the thought.

It didn't happen in the next few hours, though. After the auction, Nash went back to the car and brought a duffle bag from the trunk.

"There's someplace for us to change in the stable," he said, as he led us into a cavernous barn and on to a series of workrooms in a wing off the room with the horse stalls. The last in line was a well appointed office and tack room.

"Change?" I asked.

"Yes," Grant answered. "We going to play dress-up for the next stops."

The next stops.

We were all nearly naked and ready to put on the smart dinner clothes they were providing, knowing my sizes precisely—tailored trousers, light cashmere turtle-neck sweaters, and camel-hair jackets—when Nash, who I couldn't help but noticing was hard, muttered, "Fuck it, my balls ache from waiting," and pushed me down on my knees in front of him. "Suck it."

"Here? Won't we be seen? Does the stable owner—?" It wasn't that I was unwilling. It just was all so open.

"I own the stable, and who the fuck cares if we're seen?"

"You said you were interested in exhibitionism." The voice came from behind me. Grant. They'd read my profile closely. Maybe too closely, I thought.

It almost unhinged my jaw to take Nash in my mouth. But take him I did. I even took him when, like the stallion earlier, his cock elongated significantly as I gagged, trying to deep throat it. He placed his hands on the back of my head and guided the face-fucking motion. Grant came in close behind me, rubbed his hard cock on my neck and cheeks from behind, and reached down and twisted my nipples with his fingers, while I writhed between them and, after several minutes, took Nash's cum in my throat.

* * * *

Dinner was nearby, still in the Northern Virginia hunt club region, but in Paris. Not Paris, France. Paris, Virginia. We ate a gourmet meal in a former plantation house, turned country restaurant, the Ashby Inn. The host and waiter seemed to know Grant and Nash well—either that, or they were expertly trained to treat all guests that way. As they treated me well too, it might have been the latter.

We lingered over the meal, wine, port, and coffee. The discussion was about all things other than sex. I could have been out for an evening with well-heeled and well-informed museum colleagues with both an interest in and expertise in all things art, history, and sports. I wondered if, at the end of dinner, this will have been it and I'd be driven back to the city. I'd given them both sex. But, then, Grant had said that Nash would ride and breed me, which hadn't happened yet. But it already was getting late, past ten.

Nash had pulled the car off onto a dirt road through a grove of trees before we'd left the horse stable property.

This is it, I thought. They were going to fuck the shit out of me here and leave me for dead.

"Another change of clothes," Grant said as he was climbing out of the Mustang and Nash was popping the trunk. "We're going clubbing."

This time I was given tight leather trousers with a laced crotch flap that would drop and could be pulled all the way back through my legs and relaced on the waistband behind, leaving both equipment and hole exposed and

121

accessible. The two men had identical pants. And all three of us had mesh athlete T-shirts for on top. And black leather boots. We were triplets. But we wouldn't be triplets for long.

Nash drove the Mustang back toward Washington, D.C., getting off Route 66 at the Route 28 access to Dulles International Airport. The club was in a warehouse district abutting a runway fence of the airport and down an industrial-district road. Everything in the area looked deserted except for the parking lot of the club, which turned out to be a full-scale gay club.

We saddled up to a bar in a big room where music was blasting, a dance floor was jiving and being bombarded with a laser light display, and off to the side, under a lower ceiling and clouds of smoke, several pool tables were in use.

As I drank the beer Grant handed me and leaned back into Nash's lap, he on the stool and me between his legs, I scanned the room. Nash held me to him possessively with his palm pressing where my groin met the inner top of my left thigh. My attention focused on two black bulls playing pool at one of the tables. Clothing was optional in the room, and neither one of them wore any. Their tall, big-boned, muscular frames were magnificent, their half hards were horse hung—even larger if there was something larger on that scale.

Grant, who was sitting on a stool beside us, facing us, a hand on my basket, sensed I was getting excited about something from what he could feel in my crotch. He scanned the room too. "Who do you see, Ty? Who out there do you want? Ah, those two black bulls at the pool table?"

"Yes," I answered in a whisper. I'd never been fucked by a black man before, let alone by a black bull.

"Maybe later," Grant said, "but we're going to the movies now."

"We're leaving the club already?" I asked.

"You sound so disappointed. No, we're not leaving the club. They have an old-style porn movie house right here."

And indeed they did, all with the old theater seating in front of a stage backed by a movie screen. The curved rows of theater seats were set with more than the usual room for legs—or whatever. As we entered, a dancer was just leaving the stage, carrying his feather boa and G-string in his hand, the lights were going down lower, and a movie was coming up on the screen.

A male-on-male-on-male heavy porn movie, of course.

Grant and Nash were sitting on either side of me in a row about half way to the screen. As the movie got under way, Nash was pulling my mesh T over my head and Grant was working the leather trousers down off my legs. So much for us being triplets in our clothes. I wasn't dressed in anything for the rest of the evening at that club.

"Nash is gonna blow you and then fuck you hard now," Grant whispered in my earn. I just moaned my acquiescence and anticipation.

I could barely see what was going on on the movie screen for what was going on in the seating row we were in. There were men—couples mostly—scattered about the room in various stages of cock sucking and copulation. Grant and Nash wasted no time in catching up with them—with me. They had their hands and tongues all over me. Their heads bobbed around between my line of sight and the movie screen until Nash had moved his face down my belly and his mouth onto my cock. Grant was up on his knees in the seat next to me, his arms around my neck, pulling my head back by grabbing and pulling on the hair at the back of my head, his face over mine, taking my mouth with his in deep, tongue penetrating kisses.

Nash sank to the floor between my legs—showing why there was extra spaces between the rows. One after the other, he lifted my legs and hooked them on the seat arms. His hands were clutching my buttocks, rolling my rump up to Nash's searching tongue, which had found my asshole. When his mouth left my cock, Grant's hand replaced it and he slow-stroked me.

"You listed a movie house fantasy," Grant whispered to me when he'd come out of the kiss. He was still holding my head and torso arched back, my head over the seat back with one arm around my neck while he stroked my cock with the hand of the other arm.

I winced as Nash's tongue at my hole was replaced with one search finger, then a second, then a third.

"Open to him. You'll want to be as open to Nash as you can be," Grant whispered. "Remember the white stallion we saw. Think of Nash as that white stallion, putting all of that up inside you. Breeding you."

I could see in my peripheral vision that other men were gathering around now, sensing a show to come.

Grant was right. I wanted to be open to Nash even wider than I was when he rose up into a crouch, placed the bulb of his thick, thick cock at my rim, and started working his way inside me. I writhed and cried out at the impossibly thick, increasingly long invasion, but two men taking me held fast, Grant at my head, Nash holding my legs up and out from the arms of the seat. Other men moved in to help him—to pull my legs up almost to beside my ears, pulling my body up the seat back, drooping my head more over the back of the seat.

Men helped pin my arms down, as Grant scrambled over the back of the bank of seats, cupped my ears with hands on both side, and slid his cock into my mouth.

In to the hilt now, deep inside, still expanding, channel-splitting wide, Nash started to pound my ass in long, deep slides. And then faster and harder thrusts. Grant continued to face fuck me. All around men were groaning and egging Grant and Nash on—and expressing interest in joining them.

I strained at taking Nash. I soared to the heights at taking Nash. To the extent I could, I met his thrusts with counterthrusts and we settled into a mutually satisfying rhythm that led to an ejaculation from each of us.

Nash slurped out of me and fell back into the seat next to mine. He was still fully clothed except for the open flap at the crotch from which his still-throbbing, now-gigantic cock protruded. Grant came down in the seat on the other side of him.

I could see that Nash's cock—of such circumference and length that I still was amazed I had taken it—was dripping with cum. To show him I'd appreciated the taking, I slipped down on the floor between his spread knees and cleaned his cock with my mouth.

"Thanks," he said, with a laugh, "but you're missing the movie."

I returned to my seat, but now I saw that Grant had his cock out and was holding it in his hand. I still didn't see the rest of the movie, because, with a hand on the back of my neck, Grant was forcing me to bend over the arm of the seat and slide my lips down his cock.

So, this is what a three-man date is like, I thought. Double the attention. As soon as one is finished, the other one wants attention. I could see how such a date would be highly taxing.

Grant left the theater before Nash and I did. It wasn't long before I found out why.

When Nash told me it was time for us to go and we exited the theater, he led me further into the club complex rather than back to the main bar room. We went down a corridor with doors to rooms on either side spaced at intervals to indicate same-sized rooms of about eighteen feet in width. The sounds I heard coming from inside the doors of some of these rooms left little doubt that these were rooms for private sex sessions.

The room Nash ushered me into was obviously that. The walls, ceiling, and floor were all a dull black. Prominent in the room were two blue vinyl cube platforms I knew to be called the Liberator—cubes with wedge shapes in the form that aided the angle of penetration during sex. Many such devices had restraints attached to them. These two did. The one in the center of the room was of an elaborate configuration. The one off to the side was simpler in surface structure.

These weren't the only prominent furnishings in the room. Grant, of course, was there. But so were the black bulls I had admired playing pool in the main room. That's where Grant had gone—to enlist the aid of the black bulls. I sensed that I might begin to hyperventilate, so I concentrated on light-pant breathing.

"Lay down on the center cube, Ty," Grant said.

"What?"

"We're all going to fuck you. Your fantasy of black bulls and gang bangs—of bondage and double penetration—with the help of these big bruisers, we're going to fulfill several of your fantasies."

Double penetration. By black bulls. Oh shit.

"Or do you want the date to be over?" he asked. It was a challenge. At several junctures like that, I was offered an out. I would never know if they were serious with the offer, as I never took it. If this was going to be my one "do it all" day, I would suspend all fear and take it.

"Which way do you want me to lie on the cube?" I asked.

He showed me. I was on my back, my head toward the lower incline of a wedge shape and resting on a head rest attached at one end. My wrists went into restraints on the sides of the wedge. The other end of the cube flared out, with side pieces that, when my legs were strapped to them, were raised, spread wide, and bent below my knees, stretching, raising, and bending my legs. I felt like I was going to give birth—except I knew something very big was going to be going in rather than coming out. The edge of the wedge at that end inclined sharply so that my butt resting on it was rolled up.

Meanwhile, Grant was lowering his belly on the cube to the side, his arms and legs being strapped into restraints on the sides of the cube, his butt end at the top of a steeper incline at the back of his cube, which was lower in the middle. His torso was raised a bit on an incline in the other direction. He had been stripped naked. The black bulls already were naked, just as they were at the pool table, but now they were in full erection, licking their lips, moving around the room on the balls of their feet like gliding panthers, waiting for the action to begin, ready to pounce at a signal of release.

After Nash handed around bottles of lube and strings of Magnum packets, the fun began. Nash stripped, saddled up behind Grant, covered Grant's body with his, worked his cock inside Grant, and began to fuck him. I turned my head toward them and tried to concentrate on what they were doing rather than that there was a black bull between my legs working my hole with his lubed fingers and, as I writhed, huffed and puffed, and yielded an occasion expletive and scream, continually urged me to open to him.

"You wanna be more open for this, bitch," he muttered.

When I could feel the knuckles of his hand pressing at my rim, with the four fingers inside me, he seemed satisfied. I struggled against the restraints, arched my back, and cried out to the ceiling, as he worked his cock inside me. Thank god my first black bull was the lesser hung of the two—not that it made much difference.

When he was in and starting to pump, the other black bull came around to my head and dropped the headrest, causing my head to arch back. He grabbed my ears, forced, his cock inside my mouth, managing to get deep because of the angle of my head, and slow pumped my throat. I had to loosen my jaw to take him.

When he pulled out, I understood that relief wasn't in order, because he was smiling and rolling a Magnum onto his cock. He moved out of sight, I felt the other black bull pulling out of me, and the second took over fucking me. The first black bull went over to the other cube and relieved Nash. Nash came over to me and took up the face fuck station at my head. Reaching over my torso, he encased my cock in a hand and started jacking me off.

I came for him fairly quickly, being right on the top edge of arousal at what was happening.

After a good fifteen minutes of pumping inside me, the biggest black bull jerked and filled the bulb of his condom. He pulled out of me and went over to the other cube, where black bull one was still stroking inside Grant's ass. He grabbed Grant by the hair, lifted his head, and pushed his cock inside Grant's mouth. Grant deep-throated him for a few minutes and then pulled his mouth back and was sucking hard on the bulb. Both black bulls unloaded at nearly the same time.

Meanwhile Nash had freed me from the restraints and lowered the leg pieces, but he came up on the surface of the cube, pushed his knees under my buttocks, entered my now-gaping hole with his thick cock—which I could now take easily after the reaming by the black bulls—embraced me close, possessed my lips with his, and pistoned my channel hard. He wasn't wearing a condom, and I knew when he had creamed me deep inside.

"Whooee, love barebacking you, Ty," he murmured. "Glad you requested it."

I didn't remember requesting it. But it was glorious. I just hoped . . .

He left me and I lay there, exhausted and watching the other cube as the black bulls finished with Grant. When they had done so, they freed him, he hobbled off the cube, and the bigger of the two turned and said, "We're ready for him."

Ready for me?

Grant and Nash both moved me over to the other cube and the smaller black laid on it on his back, his cock hard again and jutting up to the ceiling.

"Ride the cock," Grant commanded, and I dutifully crawled over his waist, facing him, and, with Grant's help, lowered my channel on his cock.

I didn't have time for more than a dozen rises and falls on the cock, when he was enveloping me in his arms and pulling my chest down to his, which rolled my buttocks up . . . and which gave the other black bull the right angle to saddle up behind me and start working his cock into my channel on top of his buddies. He was the one who stroked me, while I went from weeping and crying out for mercy to whimpering and groaning to near semiconsciousness.

Afterward I lay there, sprawled on the cube, moaning and whimpering, while the four of them chatted, reviewed what they'd done, and said their good-byes.

The two black bulls left the room, and I moaned in reviewing what had been done to me in this room, both shocked and exhilarated by it. I'd done it. I'd taken two cocks at once. If I never did so again . . .

But then I realized that Grant and Nash were approaching me with big grins. Grant lay on his back at the end of the cube, his feet on the floor, me on top of him, facing away, my channel sheathing his cock. The palms of Grant's hands were clutching my pecs. Nash approached from in front of me, reaching down and grabbing my ankles, wishboning my legs, pushing his pelvis between my thighs, screwing that thick, thick, thick cock inside me on top of Grant's. And beginning to pump. As he pumped, he reached between us, fisted my cock, and began to stroke it in the rhythm of the fuck.

"Want you to remember DPing real good," Grant muttered.

* * * *

"Good for you. You passed the tests."

"Tests? What tests?" I asked Grant, turning my face to him. The three of us were sitting on the Liberator cube he'd been fucked on—that I'd been double fucked on. The incline wedges at either end of the cube had been lowered so that the surface was flat. We had showered in a bathroom connected to this room and put our party clothes back on—the leather pants and boots and the mesh T-shirts.

"You apparently are game for just about anything," he said. "You didn't flinch, even from the DP."

"I was curious," I answered. "And I've been frustrated with vanilla. It doesn't mean that I do this every day."

"You wouldn't be willing to do it again?" Grant asked, taking a sharp look at me.

"I didn't say never again," I answered, defensively.

"But has the date lived up to your expectations?"

"In spades, yes," I answered. "Are we driving back to D.C. now?"

"We could do that . . . unless you wanted to earn $400 for some more of the same and something even more tonight."

"You don't have to pay me, you know," I said. "The paperwork I signed said the date could go to dawn."

"We wouldn't be paying you. There's another club. They'll pay if you'll go on stage—let men use you in the act.

It would be similar acts to the sex acts we've done. But on stage, with a select clientele watching."

"Ah, the exhibition part."

"That part and others. Something you haven't done yet. Perhaps even something you've never thought of doing. Not life threatening, of course. If this is a one-time shot for you to experience it all, as you've told us was your interest in this date, you haven't experienced it all yet."

"$400 did you say?" That would cover my subscription to the dating site, my end of the bid on Grant and Nash, and another couple of bids if I decided to do this again before the subscription ran out. But what were the chances I'd do it again? It had been far more taxing and degrading than I had imagined it would be. I thought back to the sexual rut I'd been in before, how much pleasure and spilling of seed I had experienced already in acts I'd never considered doing before. "Just to dawn?" I asked.

"Just to dawn. The other club's about a thirty-minute drive from here. You'd be driven home."

The other club was a bit more than a thirty-minute drive, back to the Beltway around Washington, to the Maryland side, and then in toward D.C. again, from the north, on Wisconsin Avenue. Several blocks in from the Beltway, the Mustang turned right into what seemed to be an alley in a residential community of large mansions and then turned left into an underground garage. The garage was cavernous. As we'd entered, I looked at what was above it: extensive grounds, now cloaked in darkness, and an imposing Tudor-style mansion. The garage seemed to take up all of the ground under the entire property. The garage wasn't filled, by any means, but there were quite a few expensive cars parked there, most gathered around an elevator shaft.

When the elevator stopped rising and the doors opened, I realized, with a shock, that Grant didn't remind me of a fox after all. Grant was a form of satyr. The realization hit me because we were greeted in a marble foyer—floor, walls, and ceiling, all deeply veined ochre marble—by a pair of satyrs.

They were more like satyrs than Grant was, but he was close. All that he lacked were the small horns they had peeking out of their hair at the temples, goatees, horse tails, and the semblance of cloven feet. Grant shared with them the sensual, sneery smile, the pointed ears, the curved-up perpetual hard on, and the body hair, most notably the hairy legs, natural in Grant's case, a form of chaps in the case of the welcoming satyrs. The chaps were held up by a waistband which also provided the base for their horse tails. Their cloven feet were largely an illusion. They were wearing wedge heels, with the wedge being made out of clear acrylic. This forced them to walk on their toes in shoes fashioned like hooves.

"This is Ty, who has agreed to perform tonight. Please take him to Xavier." This was spoken by Grant.

Standing next to him, Nash put a hand on my arm and slid it down to take my hand. There was a calling card palmed in his hand, which I palmed, slid into a pocket of my leather pants, and later found to have a telephone number written on it. Our eyes met, and he said, "Good-bye, Ty. I really enjoyed you."

The two stepped back in the elevator, the doors closed, and they were out of my life for that evening.

"Please come with me, Mr. Ty," one of the satyr's said. He minced off toward a door on a side wall of the foyer, rather than the double doors that were directly across from the elevator, and I followed him.

I was taken to a dressing room. There were several dressing tables at one end of the room, with strong lights shining in bulbs all around the edge of a mirror covering nearly the entire wall. Clothes racks were spread around at haphazard angles with costumes on some of them—mostly satyr gear and hangers with skimpy shorts and vests in

132

forest colors. Some of the racks had a variety of street clothes hanging from them, no doubt the clothes of the performers. In the middle of the space was a brown-leather divan. Like the cubes in the other club, there were restraints attached along the sides of the divan and there was a wedge at the end facing the dressing tables and mirror walls that rose to near the bottom edge of the divan. In the space before the end of the divan were circular depressions. It didn't need much imagination to know that knees went in there.

"Xavier will be with you shortly," the satyr said. As he withdrew from the room, he added, "Strip all of our clothes off, please. Receive Xavier naked, standing up, full frontal to the door. You are being judged." I could hear the sound of an audience cheering and clapping somewhere in the not-too-far distance, as he exited and closed the door behind him.

"Shortly" was almost immediately. The satyr who entered nearly filled the room by his presence. This was an impossibly tall—surely almost seven feet tall—big-boned, and muscular satyr. Thus far all of the satyrs I'd seen had been small or regular-sized men and more willowy of figure than muscular. This one stood out as a symbol of power and strength, and, from the size of his erect, upturned cock, imposing equipment. Xavier.

"You look good. Let us see how well you will perform," he said, as he strode to me and manipulated me, despite my shocked and ineffectual attempt at struggling or at least slowing down the inevitable. He pushed me down onto the divan, bound my wrists to the sides and my ankles as well. My buttocks was rising toward the end of the divan.

There was no ceremony or preliminary, and I soon was too busy crying out and grunting and groaning to try to reason with him. He came up on the divan, his knees going into the circular depressions, his hands pressing down on the hollows where my arms met my trunk, and his cock thrust inside my ass, lifting me up off the surface of the divan as far as the restraints would allow, and with a cry to the ceiling, he began pumping me immediately in long, strong strokes. I could feel on my knees and see in the mirror that his long horse's tail was swishing back and forth to the rhythm of his stroking.

He took me swiftly, brutally, never decreasing the pistoning of his stroke, occasionally lowered his face to mine for a brutal kiss on the mouth and then down to chew my nipples, as I strained against the restraints and moaned. But after that first shocked scream of the mammoth cock striking deep inside me, I steeled myself against begging for mercy or letting him hear me cry out.

He stroked me off expertly and quickly with a fist while he fucked me and muttered, "Good, a strong arc," when I came for him.

He barebacked me, and when he came, with a jerk and a lurch and a little cry of his own, his tail went wild in its swishing. He blasted me six times—a rear back, a thrust inside, a blast of cum, a frantic swish of the tail, a rear back, a thrust inside, a blast of cum, a frantic swish if the tail, and repeat, and repeat, and repeat, and again. By the fourth blast, I had collapsed, and just lay there, murmuring, "Oh, God yes. Give it to me," begging "Again. Again," with each creaming.

I didn't pretend that I didn't love what he'd done to me.

Immediately after the last blast, he gave me a big grin, rose off my body, slapped me on the belly, muttered, "Excellent," and went to the door. He turned to me and said, "You are one of the rare ones who takes it stoically. Bawling and cursing is entertaining, but our audiences like to see our forest boys react differently. Still, one tip: Be entertaining and it will go better for you. Giving into it gradually out there will create an illusion the audience will love."

He turned away from me and opened the door. "He will do fine," he said to whoever was on the other side. "Clean him up, dress him, and bring him to the stage."

The dressing room was a flurry of the smaller-sized satyrs then—releasing me from the restraints; helping me off the divan, with no apparent concern that Xavier's cum was flowing down my thighs when I stood; and taking me to a bathroom with a communal shower, instructing me to clean myself out well—and quickly. I was needed on stage.

It seemed that all of the staff members of the club were outfitted as satyrs. I half expected to be dressed that way too. But I wasn't. I was outfitted with not much of a costume at all—soft brown suede ankle boots with pointed toes; a Lederhosen-style pair of shorts in a flimsy material that I could see had breakaway seams and that I assumed—rightly, it transpired—wouldn't be on me for very long; a skimpy brown leather vest that didn't meet across my chest and was held in place with laces; brown leather bicep bands; a thin strap around my waist that sent a leather strip down each crease of my groin and attached to a harness at the base of my cock, holding the cock out, pressing tight enough to keep me hard, and squeezing my balls into a tight ball; and a Robin Hood-style forester cap.

This obviously was what Xavier had meant by forest boys, I thought.

Then I was led to the darkened wings of what looked to be a lit-up stage. Beyond the flying buttress curtains I could see brown columns toward the back of the stage. These decorated as trees, with dense green foliage in the branches. Also in the branches, though, I could see figures. Not satyrs but man monkeys. Tails and monkey masks and not much else on. They were moving through the branches acrobatically and in slow motion to the sound of jungle music.

But nearer to that, positioned at the edge of the stage, stood Xavier. He turned, and one of the satyrs handed me over to him with the comment, "As you have tested, the substitute for the third performer, Xavier."

Xavier held a hand out to me and said, "Come."

I couldn't help but notice that he had a flogger whip in his other hand, with many long, thin leather strands.

I let him take my hand and lead me out onto the stage of a small auditorium. The artificial grove of trees with the man monkeys swinging in the branches lined the back of the stage. At the front of the stage, a platform jutted out into the audience area, which was a semicircle of raised rows of banquettes behind small, circular-top tables. Most of the seating was occupied. I couldn't make out much in the audience because of the dim light there and the blinding light turned toward the stage, but it gave the impression of a teeming mass of men, in various stages of attention to what was going on on the stage, stages of dress, and stages of cock sucking and copulation. Satyr waiters moved among the levels with trays of drinks. The bar appeared to be at the back of the auditorium, at the top-most level.

The projecting platform was a square. Set in the middle of it, though, was a circular revolving stage. In the middle of this was a flat, leather-covered Roman-style divan, probably a later model than the one in the dressing room. This was unoccupied—for the moment.

Satyrs were roaming over the stage—big men, although not as big as Xavier. By quick count I located six of them. When picking them out I also for the first time saw the two acrylic X frames set at either side of back stage at the edges next to the wings. Like the center, projecting stage, each of these was set on a revolving circle.

Hanging from these frames, by wrist and ankle restraints on the four arm extensions, the cross of the X being at the level of the shoulder blades, were two young men. Both were dressed just as I was, except that their shorts had already been pulled away. Each was being fucked in the ass by a satyr standing behind them and flogged on the chest and thighs by another satyr when they revolved around to full frontal.

Now that I knew they were there, I could separate the sounds they were making from the other sounds around me. The one on the right side of the stage was writhing to the extent his bonds permitted and was crying out and bawling like a baby. The one on the left side of the stage just hung forward on his X frame, head lowered toward the ground and whimpering.

Xavier led me out to the footlights of the platform projecting into the auditorium, where two tall, muscular satyrs were waiting for me between the footlights and the revolving inset. With a sneery smile at me, Xavier handed me over to the two satyrs. To a cheer from the portion of the audience that was paying attention, they whipped my shorts off, exposing my half hard cock, which the two, coming close to either side of me alternated working with a hand with kneading my buttocks and opening my hole with lubricated fingers. Both were sheathed with condoms—there was a profusion of both condom packets and used condoms littering the floor of the stage.

Remembering Xavier's advice, I struggled ineffectually with them, refused to turn as they wanted until they'd slapped my thighs, butt, and cock, and generally acted as if I wasn't there by my own free will.

There, after a period of preparing me—working my cock and ass, taking turns in kissing me and pushing me down on my knees to suck their cocks, before pulling me up for more work on my hole, they lifted me off the floor, sandwiched me between them, and fucked me together, one entering me from the front and the other from the rear as I writhed between them, my legs hooked on the hips of the satyr facing me.

I wasn't being stoic about this. I was screaming my bloody head off. A good part of that was ecstasy. The black bulls—even Grant and Nash—had been bigger inside me. The audience was noisy too, voicing its approval and egging the satyrs on.

When they were done, they guided me onto the revolving stage and then to the divan, where I was laid on my back and my wrists and ankles were bound by long leather leads to the sides of the couch. The two satyrs left me then, trading off with the pair of satyrs assaulting the young man on the X frame to the right of the couch.

Those two new satyrs came to the divan. One worked his way under my back, lifted my hips, and set my channel down on his up-curved cock. The other satyr moved in between my spread legs, thrust his cock inside me above that of the first satyr, and the approving audience was entertained with yet another form of double fuck.

I took this with a little less histrionics than the first double fuck. Some of that was put on. I kept thinking of Xavier's "Be entertaining" tip. As long as they thought they were taxing me to my edge of endurance maybe they wouldn't be prompted to come up with something more painful. And if I reacted with a bit less strain with each taking, maybe the audience would appreciate that. I was that much interested in the exhibitionist aspect of this experience now that I was wholly into it.

When the third set of satyrs came to me from the other X frame, I was unbound, Turned face down, my channel skewered on the cock of a satyr now lying on his back under me on the divan, restrained again, and sixth satyr came in behind me, thrust his cock inside me above that of his comrade, and pumped me to an ejaculation.

This time, I moved my hips with them, throwing my head back and screaming "Yes. Fuck me. Fuck me! Drill that hole," joining in the spirit of the fuck. The audience went wild at seeing me become actively involved in the act.

After the three exhibitions of a double penetration fuck for a appreciative audience, I was half comatose;

blubbering, but not necessarily in a bad way; and had come with each separate taking. Each time the satyrs had managed to turn me toward the audience so that it could see me spout, which was met with a cheer each time.

The three "taker" performers were rotated, with me, first, on the X frame to the right of the stage, and then to the left, as each of the other two young men were taken—a second time, I surmised—through the succession of double fucks. Throughout the performance, Xavier walked around the stage, swishing his flogger, and punishing any performer, forest "boy," satyr, man monkey who was within distance of the flick of his whip.

While the third forest "boy" was being taken on the divan, the four satyrs fucking and flogging the other forest "boy" and me withdrew and the men monkeys came down from the trees and tormented us, pinching our nipples; slapping our cocks; squeezing, distending, and crushing our balls; fingering our asses; and fucking us from behind.

I was the finale. The satyrs carried the forest "boys" off the stage and to the showers. The men monkeys swept off as well, leaving just Xavier and me on the divan, under a single strong spotlight, where he fucked me interminably in a variety of exotic positions that had the audience on its feet and clapping.

When I was dressed again in the party clothes I'd worn to the club, I was led, walking very gingerly to an office, where Xavier, now dressed in a silk robe, sat behind a desk.

"Please sit," he said, as I was led in. With some effort I lowered myself in a chair facing his desk.

"You did very well tonight . . . Ty, is it? The procurers selected and prepared you well."

The procurers. So, Grant and Nash weren't just a pair of randy and kinky men looking for a third on the dating service. They had set out to procure a performer for the show here at this club from the beginning. I tried to build up a resentment, but I couldn't. This had been the fulfillment of a fantasy. I was in pain now, but I had been aroused beyond my wildest dreams and couldn't separate the pain from the pleasure. I didn't want to separate the pain from the pleasure. I would relive this for some time to come. I might even seek it out again.

He was handing over five hundred-dollar bills. I'd only been promised four hundred, but I wasn't about to quibble over an overpayment. I don't know if I would have carried through with this added offer if Grant had told me all that it entailed.

"This show goes on every Saturday night," he said. "You did well enough to be a permanent performer—for as long as you like."

"I don't know . . . I don't think—"

"We pay $1,500 a night," he said.

$1,500, I thought. So those fuckers maybe kept $1,000 for themselves for tonight. But then there had been expenses in getting me here—and in finding me on the dating service.

"Just sign this contract, and I'll have someone drive you home. You live near Dupont Circle, don't you? And a car will pick you up there at 1:30 a.m. next Saturday."

When I entered my apartment, I went straight to my computer and brought up the dating service Web page. I was denied access to Grant and Nash's page. I wasn't surprised. I knew that capability came with membership. I knew they didn't have to recruit me a second time. But I had wondered if they might want to take me out on a date separate from the satyr club deal sometime. I can't believe that all we had done together was just a job to them.

The satyr club experience had been the icing on the cake—all of those acts I said I was curious about and I hadn't mentioned being fucked by satyrs. It was quite some experience, though.

And the date before that with Grant and Nash had been something too. But now I couldn't . . . but, yes, I could. I could contact Nash, at least. He had slipped me his telephone number. Maybe one of these days . . .

* * * *

Sunday night was missionary position night with Fraser. The obligatory fuck went as always, although I yearned for more than just the long cock deep inside me—especially now that I'd experienced so much more.

We stretched out on the bed, me cuddled into his front, his arm over me, his cock flaccid inside me, as always. And as always, after I heard his breath setting a regular pattern, I lifted his arm off me, slipped out from underneath him, and went into the kitchen for a cup of coffee.

When I returned, he had turned on his back, and as before, I had the urge to come down between his spread legs and take his cock into my mouth. "Fuck it," I said. Tonight would be a little bit different. There was no reason not to try to break this out of its routine. Fraser was quite attractive and sexy enough—especially in the semidark—and he had that impossibly long cock. He was worth the effort.

I came down between his thighs, slid my mouth down the length of his cock as I glided my hands up to this nipples, and started to suck. He responded to me. Moaning even before he came awake. Reaching down and guiding my head as I gave him deep head. Groaning and moving his hips in the rhythm of the fuck.

I rose up his body, saddled myself on his cock, and rode him as he grew thicker, longer, harder inside me and started to buck back. He was groaning and telling me how good it was, luxuriating in the exotic—for him—fuck until he couldn't take any more. With a roar, he pushed me off him, ran an arm under my stomach, lifted me up, pushed his knees under my buttocks, and snaked his cock back up into me, while, being supported by his arm encircling my waist, I cantilevered backward, arms dangling at my sides and head thrown back, concentrating all of my sensations on the cock thrusting again and again up into my passage and his hand fisting and stroking my cock. Seeking, working toward, a found mutual ejaculation.

Afterward, embracing me from behind, he declared what a surprisingly good fuck that was and how aroused he was by the variety of it. Could we fuck like that more often?

I assured him that we certainly could, myself fully satisfied with him for the first time and looking forward to progress in that direction.

He leaned his lips to my ear and whispered, "We've never done it before, but what I really would like now—"

"Yes you can fuck me again," I answered, turning my face away from him so that he couldn't see my wide grin.

Blame It on the GPS

"Hi, Bernie, this is Ramon," Morris said, introducing the hunky thirty something Latino he had walked onto the court with to his old friend Bernie. "Ramon will be your partner and James will be mine. James seems to be running late," he added.

Ten minutes earlier Bernie had seen Ramon and Morris kissing behind the small changing room when he was wandering about killing time. He was always early. Ramon was supposed to be Bernie's partner for tennis and then a meal and whatever else. It was one of Morris' regular double date arrangements. Morris and James were the other pair for the date. Bernie was more than pleased with Ramon, but he wondered if Morris might suddenly change the pairings. He had done that before. In fact, Morris seemed to like double dates, as it gave him the choice of two men instead of one. Bernie sometimes wondered why he went along with the deal, but he knew it was because Morris always produced good-looking men. Unfortunately, they were not always too smart, but Bernie had met a couple of men he had had long-term relationships with through Morris. The last relationship, which had seemed special, was in the throes of ending. Hence his appearance at the court today

The three began to hit the ball. Ramon obviously was a very mediocre tennis player but looked very good doing it.

"James is really coming?" Bernie asked after they had been hitting the ball around for ten minutes.

"Sure, I checked this morning," said Morris. "How about you come and play on my side, Ramon," he added. "Practising against both of you is exhausting."

Bernie was a bit annoyed as Ramon trotted to the other side of the net. But he had seen it coming, and as they continued to hit the ball around, he had a better view of Ramon.

Bernie was so busy hitting balls back and watching Ramon that the fourth man was through the gate and on the court before he saw him.

"What the. . . ?" Bernie started to say.

"OK, game on. Your serve, Bernie," Morris cried out.

Bernie looked daggers at Morris but went to the baseline from where he directed a serve right at his body. Morris returned it somehow and James came in to return it with a nice backhand. Morris managed to get to it and send it back to Bernie, who made a point of directing it at Ramon, who missed it by a mile.

"Good shot," the new arrival said. "Who is he anyway?"

"Ramon. Morris' man for the day. Though he was supposed to be mine, James." Bernie looked at his partner with annoyance.

The ball came back and Bernie served again, this time managing to ace Morris.

"Yes," he shouted, pumping his arm.

After that Ramon seemed to wake up and the play got tougher. Bernie and James were suddenly battling hard for each point, working together like two parts of a well-oiled machine as the game went on. Communicating with small gestures and looks.

When they finally won, Bernie and James threw themselves at each other and hugged, but only briefly before Bernie broke away and stood back. "Well played," he said as they went over and shook hands with their opponents.

"You set me up," Bernie hissed at Morris.

Morris just shrugged. "Lunch at Carlo's? All into the shower together now?"

It was a joke, as there was just one shower in the small change room building and it barely fit two, as they all knew—except perhaps Ramon.

While the four of them were showering and changing, Bernie looked Ramon over, but James got between them as he walked by, and it was James that Bernie watched then. He felt an instant charge, seeing the very nice and familiar body of the man he had made love to so often. He also realised it was a while since he had looked at it properly.

James, of course, was not James, but Tom. And Tom was Bernie's current, but almost no longer, partner.

Pulling his eyes back to Ramon, Bernie saw he was possibly better hung than Tom, but Bernie knew that Tom was a grower. And he was growing now in the change room, looking over at Bernie and seeing that he was also getting hard. Bernie picked up a towel and covered himself as he was getting fully hard. He was now unable to take his eyes off Tom as he walked into the shower, left the door open, and began to wash, his hands running lightly here and there on his body, his arms lifting, stretching out his torso, his cock standing out his hands cleaning himself. It was all Bernie could do not to join him in the shower.

Things had gone well between them until recently. But now Bernie had a new role at work and was so busy and often away, that he didn't always have time to let Tom

145

know when he would be home. And it was usually impossible for him to go to Tom's place. Then when they were together, he often didn't have the energy for more than a quick release fuck and sleep. Tom had talked about Bernie moving into his place, which was larger, so they'd have more time together, and when Bernie had not agreed, had mentioned seeing someone else because he had needs. Bernie did not want an open relationship, so . . .

When they were all sitting at a back table in Carlos', Morris dropped his bombshell. "Ramon here is a relationship counselor, and he is here to help you guys."

Bernie groaned, "Oh, no, Morris. And what is he going to do over lunch? Did you know about this, Tom?"

"I want things to work out with us, but I didn't know Morris had done anything but set up the blind date. We never get to spend time doing things together anymore and we used to enjoy tennis. I thought it might help to bring us together."

Bernie felt a twist in his gut and could have fucked Tom right there for saying that, but the problems pulling them apart had not changed. He guiltily knew a big one was his new work role, but he told himself yet again that good jobs were hard to find.

"OK, so we have not much time. Here is a list of questions you each have to answer aloud," Ramon said, as he handed each of them a sheet of paper.

Bernie read:

Where do you want to be in five years time?
Is religion important to you?

"There are only two questions," he said. "What good is that?"

"First, I want you both to tell each other, and us, where you want to be in five years time," Ramon replied.

"What sort of life you want, what job, where you want to live. Think about it for a couple of minutes."

"I . . ." Tom started to say, but Ramon shushed him. "Two minutes."

Bernie's mind was full of incoherent thoughts. He wanted too much maybe or there was nothing really important to him.

"I want to live in a house with a garden, and a special man," Tom said as soon as Ramon nodded, signaling their thinking time was up, "and a dog. I want a dog."

"You have a dog already," Bernie said. "That is why you have to keep your townhouse. You can't stay over at my flat often because of the no pet's rule, so your dog can't come."

"And you won't come to my townhouse. Is it because of my dog?" Tom asked.

Bernie looked at him in surprise. "I like Tank, you know that, but your townhouse is an extra half hour from my work. The hours I am working I don't need that extra hour commuting. That is why I don't stay there, why I can't move in. I have told you that."

"I thought it was Tank, but you didn't want to say so," Tom said, looking confused. "But I don't know why it takes you so long. The times I have gone from my place and met you at your work for lunch its only taken me twenty minutes to get there."

Bernie snorted, "in your dreams. It takes me nearly an hour."

"It can't," Tom said, looking at Bernie as if he were mad. "Straight up my street, a left, a right onto the high street and then around the park and under the motorway and along the railway line and . . ."

"What do you mean, up the high street? The GPS says the shortest route is on the motorway, and I turn right onto the high street and go along that for a mile or so and . . ."

Tom looked stunned. "The GPS is not always right, Bernie," he said, "I worked out that route myself ages ago, all empty back streets." He was reaching out a hand for one of Bernie' hands. "Is this what has been the problem between us, your GPS?"

Bernie sat back and looked at Tom as they held hands on the table. "Seriously? You do it in twenty minutes? So show me," he said, standing up.

"OK, let's go. Will we start at your office or my place?"

"The office," Bernie said, feeling a load lift off his shoulders. He knew he had been a bit of a princess on the time thing, but he was struggling to keep up with the new job and much as he loved Tom he had no energy for dealing with personal problems on top.

"Wait," Ramon said. "Before you leave Bernie has to tell us where he wants to be."

"Me, I want a job that does not exhaust me and a man who loves me like Tom does, and a dog." He meant it all, he realised, as he said it. A job should not be ruling his life to the point it was ruining his relationship and he had realised that Tom was far too good to lose. "Thanks for the tennis date, Morris," he added as he left with Tom.

Morris looked at Ramon, "That was a great result. Now I think we should celebrate. I can make you a great lunch at my place."

Ramon laughed and laid a hand on Morris' leg under the table.

* * * *

Bernie sat in his car for a minute, his eyes closed. Tom's townhouse was in front of him, and the journey from his office really had taken about twenty minutes. He opened his eyes, looked at his GPS, and slapped it hard. Then he got out of the car and joined Tom at his front door. He pressed himself up close to Tom and kissed the back of his neck as Tom got out his key and let them in.

Bernie had time to say, "I am sorry," after the door was closed and before their mouths were joined and their bodies pressed together, trying to meld into one. The first fuck was in the living room on the couch, Bernie on top, wanting to possess Tom completely, wanting to prove he was back and his. Entering him was like coming home and he felt the tension draining out of him, unable to stop himself from coming quickly. Then he stroked Tom off, murmuring, "So sorry, so sorry."

"For what?" Tom asked with slitted eyes.

"For coming first," Bernie replied, and would have added more if Tom had not spouted his cream just then and he had not lowered his mouth to lick it off.

Doubled Date

"I'm going to come!"

"If you can hold it just a bit more, I can come too," Kevin hissed.

And then we managed to come close to each other. We were lying on our backs side by side on Kevin's double bed in his apartment at U. Delaware. His place was preferable to my dorm because his bed was wider than mine and his apartment was more private than my dorm suite was. I was a freshman and he a senior. So, I had to be in the dorms; he had a studio apartment off campus.

This was the third time we'd met to jack off together. That's all we'd done so far, and even that was limited. We lay side by side, kissing and pulling on each other's cocks, but for the grand finale, we'd both be jacking ourselves.

It's not that I wasn't open to more—or hadn't had more before. I'd gotten into U. Delaware on a sports scholarship partly because of the relationship I'd had with my high school tennis coach in the previous year. It had been pretty intense there for a couple of months into the middle of the summer and then we both went our own ways—mine was a two-week fling with a construction worker. His was his wife reining him in more closely.

150

Kevin had gone to my high school—and had once been the same thing to my coach as I later was. When we first met at the tennis team practices at U.D. and he'd heard where I came from, he knew what I was interested in—and what I would do. We hit it off together and got real comfortable with each other.

The only problem was that we wanted pretty much the same thing from sex. We were both bottoms. So, here we were, making do. Maybe we'd progress to mutual blow jobs, but maybe not. It all seemed a bit incomplete.

After we'd come, I lay my head on his chest and we just settled in to cooling down and doing some fondling work with our hands.

"That released some tension," Kevin murmured. "I hope it did you good too, Nathan."

"Pretty good," I answered. And that's what it was—pretty good. Not great; just pretty good. Maybe if I hadn't had better before, I'd be more satisfied with it. But there was a lot of tension in trying to keep the grades up in my freshman year while we were in tennis competitions that spring and this at least gave me some release and relief, just as Kevin claimed it did him.

"Are you getting any otherwise?" Kevin asked. "I know it helps to blow off steam."

"Not really. Little time and opportunity," I answered. "And you?"

"Yeah, I got a guy in Wilmington who takes me all the way. He's in banking. Older guy, just past thirty. If it weren't for him, I'd be a wreck."

"It all helps, man," I said. I didn't want Kevin to think that I didn't appreciate these sessions.

* * * *

"How do you feel about blind dates?" Kevin had called me on the cell phone as I was moving from my English class to chemistry.

"Haven't ever had one."

"An old friend of Jack's is in town. We had a date, but this old friend showed up. I really need to have this date. He said that if I could find a friend for his friend—"

"Jack?"

"Yeah, the banker from Wilmington I told you about."

"Sure, why not?" I said. Bankers made good money, I thought. Beat me, though, what I was supposed to do with this friend while Kevin's boyfriend was giving him the relief he sounded over the phone like he needed. But I guess I'd find out. Kevin had said they'd spring for some sort of activity and dinner, so it couldn't be a total loss.

His name was Ed, and he wasn't a banker. Whereas Kevin's guy, Jack, had gone the professional route—and looked it, all expensively dressed, groomed, and gymed, a blond god type—Ed hadn't gone to college. He was a construction worker. He was dressed clean enough, but really casual, and he was wearing construction boots. They weren't muddy or anything, but All-American he wasn't. He was at least part Latino. Dark and sultry, to be sure, and all muscle. But, whereas Jack was a glib talker, Ed was the glowering silent type. I had no idea how these two guys had gotten together other than the old adage of opposites attracting.

But they were paying, and it was a Saturday, with all my week's classes done and a bye week in our tennis schedule. I needed the break of something else to do.

What I was finding at the beginning of this blind date, though, was mainly frustration. I found that I wanted to be dating Kevin's guy, Jack, rather than the morose and uncommunicative Ed.

As a foursome we worked out OK as we attended a Blue Rocks minor league baseball game at a small stadium on the Christiana River front on the north edge of downtown Wilmington, because Kevin and Jack dominated and made the conversation interesting. Likewise dinner at a sports bar restaurant on 202 off I-95 west of the city went OK, as well. This, if you discounted that Kevin and Jack, sitting across from me, were all hands and stolen kisses, and Ed, sitting next to me, was all his steak and potatoes. He didn't react to me laying a hand on his thigh, so I withdrew it and didn't go there again.

At Club X on Orange Street afterward, Kevin, Jack, and I went to the dance floor and flirted with the pole dancers who had come down from Philly for Saturday night, while Ed protected our table by holding it down and leaving it only for the men's room between beers.

He did give me looks every once in a while that established domination and I lowered my eyes for him to show submission, but I had no idea where this was going to lead. I certainly knew that Kevin and Jack were headed for a fuck session. They had hands all over each other all evening and were cooing. Jack was a real hunk, and I envied Kevin. And I guess that was the main feeling I was gathering from this blind double date—envy and a bit of frustration. Ed was a hunk too, but I worried on whether he'd been roped into this double date and wanted to be somewhere else altogether. The only moments of animation I saw in him was when he was talking with Jack—who would bring out the interest in anyone. I had fleeting moments of wonder if Ed even was a top, or whether he was here for interest in Jack. That would be a real bummer, I thought.

For a moment or two I had versions of the three of them, Jack taking care of both Kevin and Ed, and me sitting off to the side, unnoticed and unfucked.

And then that thought was laid to rest, at least, when Ed, who was driving Jack's car, because Jack wanted to be in the backseat with Kevin, drove us into a park and off the main drive onto a gravel side drive that led to privacy among enveloping trees.

Ed and I sat there at the opposite ends of the front seat for several minutes of awkwardness as Jack and Kevin went directly into a lap fuck in the backseat. Kevin was obviously vocal about the work of Jack's cock in his passage, which, at last, seemed to get through to Ed and arouse him. He reached over and cupped the back of my neck in a hand and pulled me to him. I thought that we were going into a kiss, but the pull continued past his face, down into his lap, where I found his dick had been freed from his fly. He was hard, and I remember marveling at how he'd managed to get hard as much of an iceberg as he had been.

It was a very nice cock, I knew what to do, and I had no better prospect at the moment, although I was aching to be in the backseat and getting what Kevin was getting. So I opened my mouth over his cock and gave him what I thought was a perfectly good blow job.

If there was going to be more from Ed, that was cut off by Jack being finished with Kevin in the backseat and suggesting to Ed that he drive him and Kevin to Kevin's apartment and me to my dorm and then Ed could pick Jack up at Kevin's apartment.

Ed was enough of a gentleman to hand me his handkerchief to clean his cum off my face before, without looking directly at me again, putting the car in gear and driving out of the park.

* * * *

Everything changed when we got to my dorm. I opened the passenger door to get out, not saying anything to Ed because I assumed we were finished and I was tired of trying to make talk—suggestive or otherwise—with him,

154

only to find him standing by the car and closing the door after I'd stepped out. He put his arm around me—which is closer than he'd gotten all day to me—and bear hugged me up the walk and into the dorm and up the stairs to my floor.

"Umm, thanks, I can take it from here," I said. "It was a nice—"

"I'm coming in. Which room is yours? Jack said you had the room to yourself."

He fucked me on my bed, taking me hard, and with little preparation. All he seemed to care about was that he was hard and was going to get his rocks off; it mattered little to him whether I was ready for him or not. As long as enough lube could be applied for him to get inside me, he seemed satisfied. He kept muttering, "Open to me. Open it up, dammit."

He didn't just want to get some of it inside me. He wanted to bottom in me, and he wasn't built small, by any means. I screwed up my eyes and took it, though, because I wanted to get fucked bad.

All the time I was doing my best to take him inside me. I did want him inside me. I wanted someone inside me bad, and he was the one who was here. He was reasonably good looking, young enough to be vigorous and have stamina, and hard bodied. I was aching to be fucked, and, once he'd gotten all of his cock inside me, he was doing a good job in that department.

Ed was straightforward and efficient. He took me in a missionary position, with a pillow under my waist, my legs spread and bent, and his weight pinning me to the bed as he lay between my legs. He held my head between his hands, his thumbs pressing up into the soft tissue under my jaw, arching my head up so that I was looking up at the ceiling as he pumped my ass hard. I understood, as I'm sure he wanted me to, that he could render me unconscious with those thumbs if I gave him the slightest resistance.

155

I didn't give him any resistance. It had been some seven months since I'd had a man's cock inside me, and I came for Ed without the least trouble. But he fucked on for maybe fifteen more minutes before he got his rocks off. He was all cold efficiency, no affection whatsoever. But he also was hard and filling, long lasting and vigorous. It wasn't heaven, but it was far enough into the clouds to be registered as a "good thing." And I came a second time before he finished. I didn't come big like I did the first time, but he was the first one I'd come twice with before he came once. Of course it had been seven months and I needed it bad.

My "date" filled the bulb of his condom with a grunt; rolled off me, stripping the rubber off in the process and tossing it in the trashcan by my desk; and was pulling on his jeans in one fluid movement. "Nice tight ass," he said, the closest to a compliment I knew I was going to get from him, and then, "I'm taking a piss; stay there. I'm not done yet."

Well, OK, that was more of a compliment. He went out of the door to my dorm room to the communal bathroom across the hallway, and I lay there, fingering my ass. I was going to be fucked again. This was my lucky day.

He was gone for several minutes—long enough for me to worry whether or not he had encountered one of my suitemates in the head and was doing him. As coldly as he had fucked me, he had gotten my hopes up that he'd spike me again when he came back. He was better than nothing—a whole hell of a lot better.

He was unzipping his jeans as he came into the room. "You're going to ride me now," he growled. He was half erect again and flopped down on the bed on his back as I sat up. I leaned over, took him in my mouth, made him erect again, rolled another condom on him at his direction, and then straddled his hips, and descended on his erection. Without so much as a "thank-you," he grabbed my waist, helped me rise and fall on the cock, and added his grunts to my groans, as my half-hard cock slapped against his belly.

I was concentrating so much on having a good time, hardening up, and getting another ejaculation out of this that I didn't notice the other guy come into the room immediately. When I did, I didn't have any trouble hardening up at all. Jack was there, in all his magnificent glory, the glory intensifying as he stripped and I saw that he was horse hung—and in erection.

He came up on the bed behind me and between Ed's legs. Ed didn't seem the bit surprised that he was there. I nearly hyperventilated as Jack cupped my biceps in his hands, leaned in and kissed me on the back of the neck, and whispered, "Have you ever been doubled before? I want to share you with Ed. We like to share our men."

No I hadn't, and I had no idea if I could manage it or not. The tennis coach was hung and he liked to put three fingers in there, slide in between them, and leave them there while he stroked me, so . . . but it didn't matter. I'd been aching for Jack all day. "Fuck me. Fuck me," I murmured in an acquiescence that didn't answer the question.

But I didn't care and he didn't ask again.

The pain was excruciating at first, and I wanted to scream out for them to stop. But Jack was possessing my lips with his and his kiss was so sweet and possessing that I never wanted it to stop or be interrupted by the issue that I wasn't really built to have two cocks in me at once. But then I started to adjust to them—and continued to adjust to them—to the point where the pleasure of the mere idea of what they were doing and what I was taking washed over me, and we became a three-piece fucking machine—all grunts and groans and sighs and moans, and, eventually, ejaculations.

I lay there, my chest on Ed's chest, Jack's chest on my back, panting when we all had come. Both of them were still inside me, but going flaccid, so the challenge of taking them both was passed. Ed was stoic and remote as before, but Jack was all affection, kissing and fondling me and whispering the language of the satisfactorily completed fuck in my ear.

I could have stayed like that forever, but it, naturally, was Ed who broke the spell, by grunting and rolling out from beneath me, leaving the bed, making another condom deposit in the trash can, and pulling on his jeans and his shirt as he stood by the bed.

Jack remained on top of me, covering me from above at full stretch. I could feel his cock reawakening inside me, and all I could think of was the "Hallelujah Chorus." He was still kissing me and his hands were running over the curves and crevices of my body. He and Ed were a study in contrasts in the attention they gave the men they were fucking. Jack could do anything to me he wanted to do.

"I'll wait for you in the car," Ed said.

"It will be a while," Jack answered.

"I figured. A sweet piece. Took us both like a champ." More compliments from Ed. Who would have known he had such compliments he was willing to spend? But who cared at the moment? Jack was on me, in me. He was going to fuck me again. This time I was going to heaven.

And I did. And I walked on the clouds.

"Can you raise your hips, go up on your knees a bit?" he murmured in my ear. "I want to give it all to you, to fuck you deep."

"Hallelujah," I actually muttered, as I presented for him and he did, indeed, fuck me long and deep. I wouldn't have cared if Ed had to wait out in the car all night—and the next day and night after that.

"I want to see you again; fuck you again," Jack whispered in my ear when he was done and we were cooling down, him still covering my body, still inside me.

"But . . . Kevin," I managed to say, although it took all of my fortitude to bring that subject up.

"Kevin needn't know. I can handle you both, if you don't mind, and Kevin doesn't have to know. That's what this blind double date was for. Ed was here as camouflage for me wanting to get at you. Kevin showed me those nude photos you sent him and I've been crawling the walls to be able to get at you. But Ed and I do like to double guys. So, what do you say? Are you good with it?"

"Who the hell is Kevin?" I responded, with a grin.

~

About the Authors

Shabbu is the combined pen name for two established authors, one on the East Coast of the United States and an Australian, until recently living on the East Coast of Australia, but now in southern Europe, who spin erotica together in cyber space.

Habu, a bisexual former supersonic spy jet pilot, intelligence agent, and diplomat, is a published mainstream novelist and short story writer under another name and in another dimension of his life.

Sabb, once an accountant and sometime property developer, is a wild barbarian at heart, who knows that love is out there of you're lucky enough to find it.

You can find habu and Sabb at their website www.BarbarianSpy.com. These authors' erotic, and nonerotic, e-novels and anthologies are published by BarbarianSpy in e-book and paperback, and available from all major on-line book retailers.

Our authors like to receive feedback and appreciate it when readers post reviews of their books at distributor and review sites.

BarbarianSpy
FOR LITERARY HEAT

Not all books listed below may currently be on release.
* indicates the book is available in paperback and e-book.

BOOKS BY CHRIS CROSS
Multisexual Adult Romance
Pulaski Square
Chocolate in Vanilla (MF)
Christmas with Chris (MMF) (MM) (MF)

BOOKS BY ALEX LOCKHEED
Transgender Romance
Meeting Jenna
Transgender Other
Being Sarah

BOOKS BY DIRK HESSIAN
Xtreme Historical Erotica
Ancient Times (Print only Bundle)*
The King's Men
Shores of Tripoli*
Prophecy of Noto
Pretender's Fate
General Historical Erotic Romance
Ridden West
Deliver a Virgin (Short)
Clouds and Rain (Short)
Confederate Gold
Puttin on the Ritz
To the Hessian Hills
Fire Down the Valley*
Constantinople*
The Beautiful Way*
Blue and Gray
Colonel's Treasure
Beginning of Time
Labyrinth

BOOKS BY HABU
Gay Erotica
Memoir Faction
Flying High, Diving Deep*
Xtreme Erotica
Fist of Gold

Liaisons
Chain Gang Banged (Short Story)
Tramp Steaming*
Escape to Girne
Silas' Choice*
Last Call
Choke Hold
Apyko: The Greek Pimp
Visits of the Schlange
Second Coming: Emile La Cour Unleashed*
Vortex: Sacrificed by Curiosity*
Dark Angel Sounding *(in e-book & included in Sounding:Ultimate Control paperback)**
Sounding: Ultimate Control *(Print Only)**
Sounding Five *(in e-book & included in Sounding:Ultimate Control paperback)**

Romance
GayLords Inn*
Finding a New Sam
Bangkok Summer Seduction
The Photograph
Inevitable Case
Turn to Love
Rain Check
Built for Pleasure (Sci Fi)
Danny's Choice*
Pull of the Groove
Sugar n Spice Christmas
Friday Nights with Lenny (Christmas Romance)
Snowy, Snowy Nights (Christmas Romance)
Tank n Bull
Sail to the Sun
War Letters
Ravens Roost
Caribbean Cruise Top to Bottom
Arena Stage
Trading Partners (Valentine's Day)
Four Coins
Lower Than the Heart (Valentine's Day)
Brambleton
Gotta Keep Trying
Finding Amnad
Platres Conclave
Other Novels/Novellas
Another Frist Time

Syrian Ram
Temptation's Clutches*
Descent into Chaos
Escape to Girne
Journey Through Abilene
Harmony and Dissonance
Stallion Station
Racing With the Devil (espionage suspense)
Prepared in Cape Verdi
Gilded Cage
House on Park*
Anything for Ambition
Dance of the Ravishers
Hard Knocks U*
My Neighbor's Spa*
Man's Man: Tales of a High Priced Gay Hooker*
Trip Money
The Indian Doctor
Sailorboy
Home to Fire Island
Murder Mysteries
All Fools Day Foolery (Mike Kavanagh)
Inevitable Case (Mike Kavanagh)
Vanishing Laura
Death on a Ping Pong Table
Clint Folsom Mysteries Compendium Volume 1*
Death to Blonds - Stolen Judgment (Clint Folsom Mystery)*
Clint Folsom Mysteries Compendium Volume 2*
Gay Erotica Anthologies
Earth Cry*
Shunga
Habu's Christmas Balls
Eight in D*
DevilMENt
Silas' Choices*
Stallion Station (A Novella in Parts)
Eleven to the Dogs*
Fifty Seventy*
Spy Tails 001*
Spy Tails 002*
Doubled*
Doubled Again*
Tails in the Tropics*
Tails in the Med*
Tails in the West*

Rough Riders*
Grab Bag 1*
Grab Bag 2*
Grab Bag 3*
Grab Bag 4*
Grab Bag 5*
Grab Bag 6*
Grab Bag 7*
Grab Bag 8*
Grab Bag 9*
Grab Bag 10*
Beyond the Beaded Curtain*
Habu's Christmas Balls
The Sporting Life*
Fetish Galore!*
Literary Gay Erotica
Cairo Surrender*
The Handyman*
Homeward Bound
Journey to Mirage*
Bisexual/Menage/Multisexual Erotica
And Eat it Too
Two Men, One Woman*
Every Which Way
Summer of Denial
Death on a Ping Pong Table
Cruising Gigolo
13 Ways for Halloween
Luther*
The Indian Prince*
BOOKS BY SABB
Driver Reliever
Hiring in Hollywood
The Legend of Holleystone Grange
Surprise Encounters*
She is He
Wrong Man
Loyal to his King
Barbarian Tales - Book One - Traveler's Tales*
Barbarian Tales - Book Two - Journeys Begin*
Barbarian Tales - Book Three - The Inheritance*
Barbarian Tales - Book Four - Road to Persepolis*
BOOKS BY SHABBU
Velvet Interrogation
Finding Jason

Dirty Pool
Operation Black Jade
Cigars!*
Angel in the Barn
Gayly Complicated*
Despoiling David
The Tree of Idleness*
I Met a Man
Rough Road to Happiness
BOOKS BY STEPHEN KESSEL
Gay Romance
The Forever Man
Two Chances
BOOKS BY KIM BLACK
Lesbian Romance
Transfixed on Tammie (F/T lesbian)